WEB TOON

LEARN TO DRAW

unORDINARY

uru ♡

Walter Foster

 T0390860

Learn to draw your favorite characters from the popular webcomic series with exclusive behind-the-scenes and insider tips!

Quarto.com | WalterFoster.com

© 2024 Quarto Publishing Group USA Inc.
WEBTOON UnOrdinary © uru-chan. Inc. All rights reserved.
WEBTOON and all related trademarks are owned by WEBTOON Entertainment Inc. or its affiliates.

First Published in 2024 by Walter Foster Publishing, an imprint of The Quarto Group,
100 Cummings Center, Suite 265-D, Beverly, MA 01915, USA.
T (978) 282-9590 F (978) 283-2742

All rights reserved. No part of this book may be reproduced in any form without written permission of the copyright owners. All images in this book have been reproduced with the knowledge and prior consent of the artists concerned, and no responsibility is accepted by producer, publisher, or printer for any infringement of copyright or otherwise, arising from the contents of this publication. Every effort has been made to ensure that credits accurately comply with information supplied. We apologize for any inaccuracies that may have occurred and will resolve inaccurate or missing information in a subsequent reprinting of the book.

Walter Foster Publishing titles are also available at a discount for retail, wholesale, promotional, and bulk purchase. For details, contact the Special Sales Manager by email at specialsales@quarto.com or by mail at The Quarto Group, Attn: Special Sales Manager, 100 Cummings Center, Suite 265-D, Beverly, MA 01915, USA.

10 9 8 7 6 5 4 3 2 1

ISBN: 978-0-7603-8981-2

Digital edition published in 2024
eISBN: 978-0-7603-8982-9

Library of Congress Cataloging-in-Publication Data is available.

Step-by-step artwork: Ryan Axxel
WEBTOON Rights and Licensing Manager: Amanda Chen
Design, layout, and editorial: Christopher Bohn, Mark Mendez, Gabe Thibodeau, and Coffee Cup Creative LLC
Copyeditor: Susan H. Greer
Illustrations and art: uru-chan and WEBTOON Entertainment, except Shutterstock on pages 26 and 27.

Printed in USA

CONTENTS

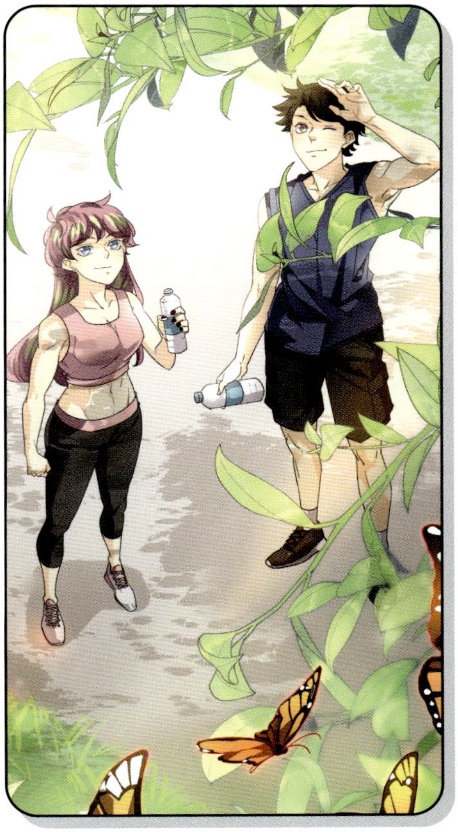

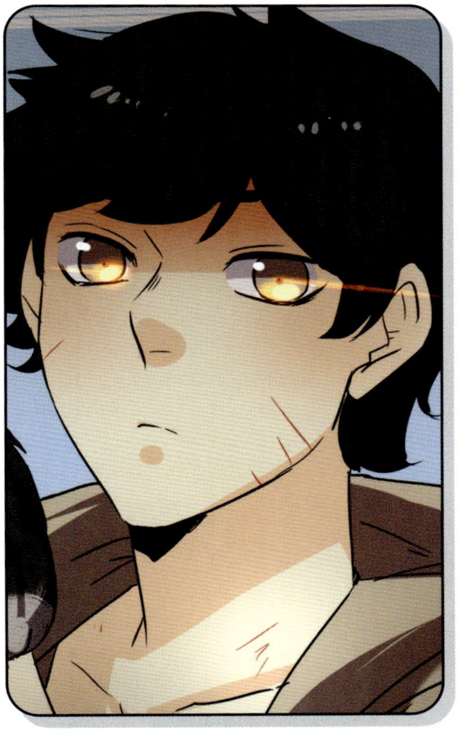

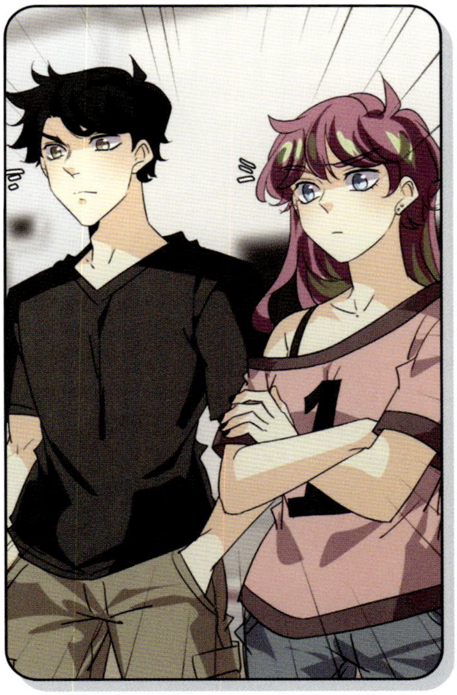

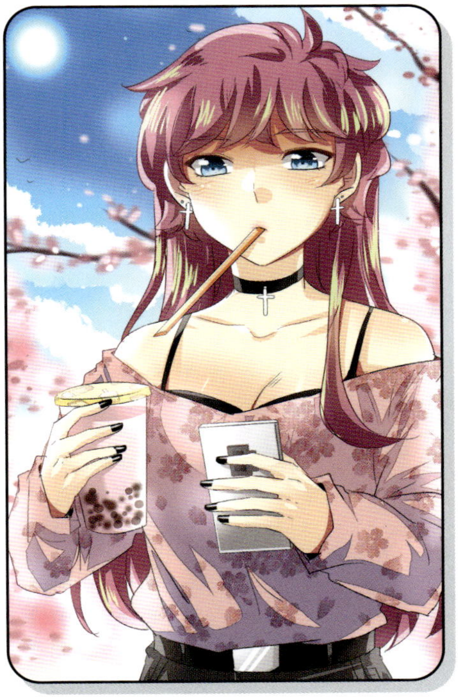

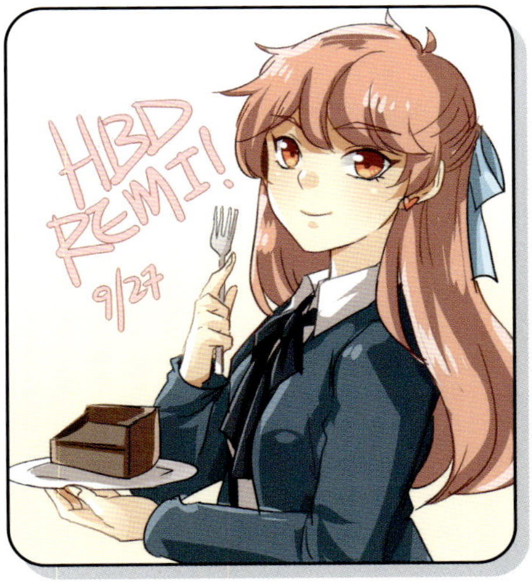

HBD REMI!
9/27

INTRODUCTION

Welcome to Wellston Private High School, an educational institution where the top students in the region gather and hone their abilities.

Uncover your own superpower drawing skills while learning to draw characters from unOrdinary, including John, Seraphina, Arlo, Remi, and more!

What Is unOrdinary?

Nobody pays much attention to John, a normal teenager at a high school where the social elite possess unthinkable powers and abilities. But John has a secret; his complicated past threatens to uproot the school's entire social order, and much more.

Check out the latest episode of the hit WEBTOON series.

SYNOPSIS

When John arrives at Wellston Private High School, he's hopeful for a fresh start, but those hopes are quickly dashed. Every student in the school possesses a superpower—except for John. Seraphina has the power to manipulate time. Arlo can form an impenetrable barrier of protection around himself. Isen, Blyke, and Remi each have their own skills as well. But John is a "weakling," and this places him squarely on the bottom rung of the school's hierarchy.

Welcome to unOrdinary life. *Learn to Draw unOrdinary* is an illustrative guide that all aspiring comic, manga, or anime artists will love. From learning to draw your favorite characters to mastering basic drawing techniques, this helpful guide is the ideal companion for artists-in-training and fans of the hit series.

What Is a Webcomic?

Webcomics are comics published on a website or mobile app.

Meet WEBTOON™.

We started a whole new way to create stories and opened it up to anyone with a story to tell. We're home to thousands of creator-owned series with amazing, diverse visions from all over the world. Get in on the latest original romance, comedy, action, fantasy, horror, and more from big names and big-names-to-be—made just for WEBTOON. We're available anywhere, anytime, and always for free.

FROM THE CREATOR

What was your inspiration behind creating your WEBTOON series?

I was inspired by a variety of genres and the desire to explore themes related to mental health, self-discovery, self-forgiveness, and philosophy. Characters' personalities were written to relate to a wide variety of readers. While designing, I knew I wanted to use very different colors and hairstyles to make each character stand out from one another.

How did you get into creating your WEBTOON series?

I'm a self-taught artist and author. I really enjoyed watching anime and reading stories growing up. My dream job was to become a mangaka, so I would draw my own stories and post them on SmackJeeves and DeviantArt in hopes of building an audience. I don't have much of a traditional art background (I actually studied engineering in school) but it just goes to show that anyone can draw their own comics!

Is there advice you would give your fans when trying to draw your characters or starting their own series?

The best way to start is to study your favorite art styles and stories! Once you have the basics down, then it's easier to move on and develop your own drawing style! Practice drawing, read a lot of stories, and watch a lot of shows! There is no shortcut to getting better. My first anime inspirations were *Yu-Gi-Oh!*, *Sailor Moon*, *Dragon Ball Z*, and *YuYu Hakusho*. Some of my favorite epics were *The Legend of the Condor Heroes*, *Journey to the West*, and *My Fair Princess*.

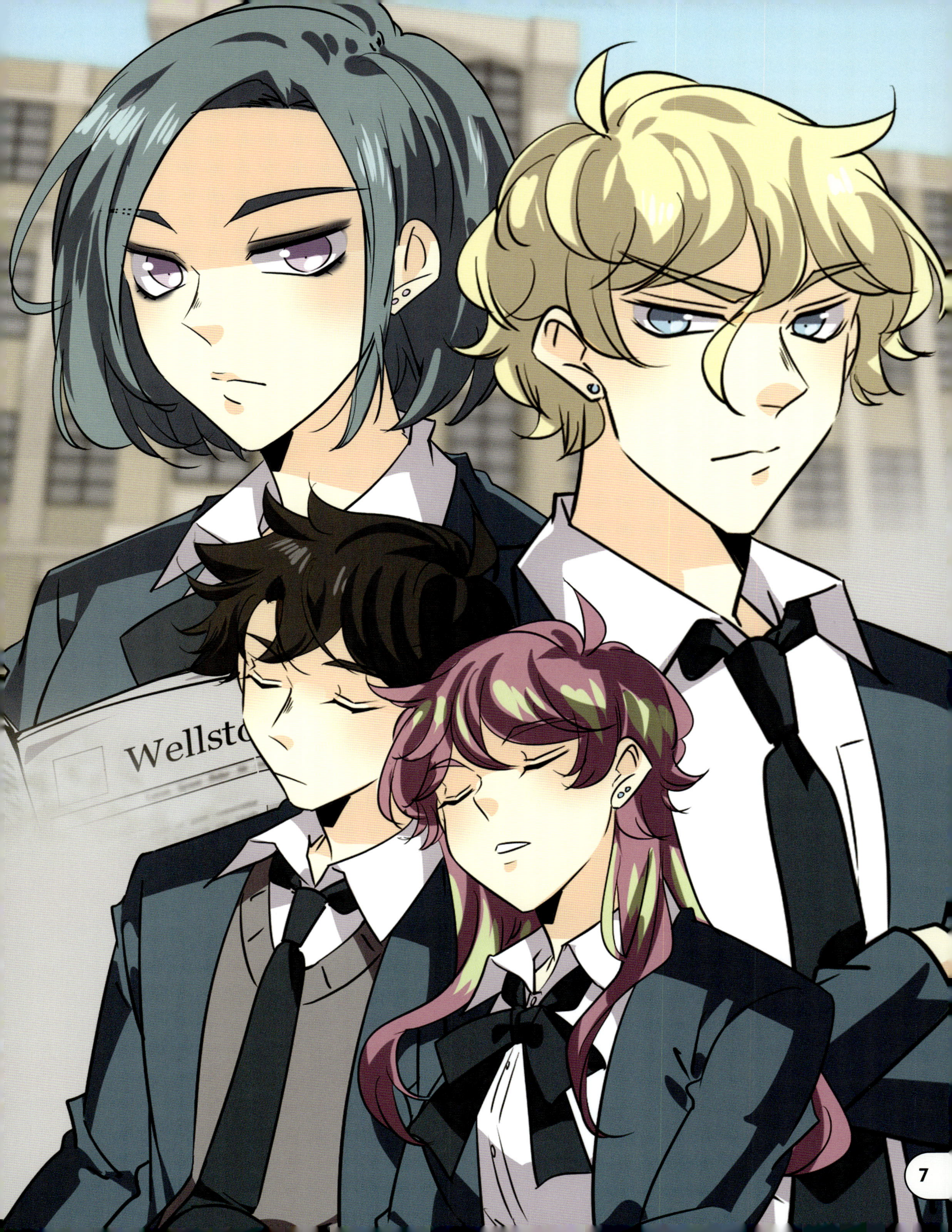
Wellst

The Characters

Meet the cast of unOrdinary!

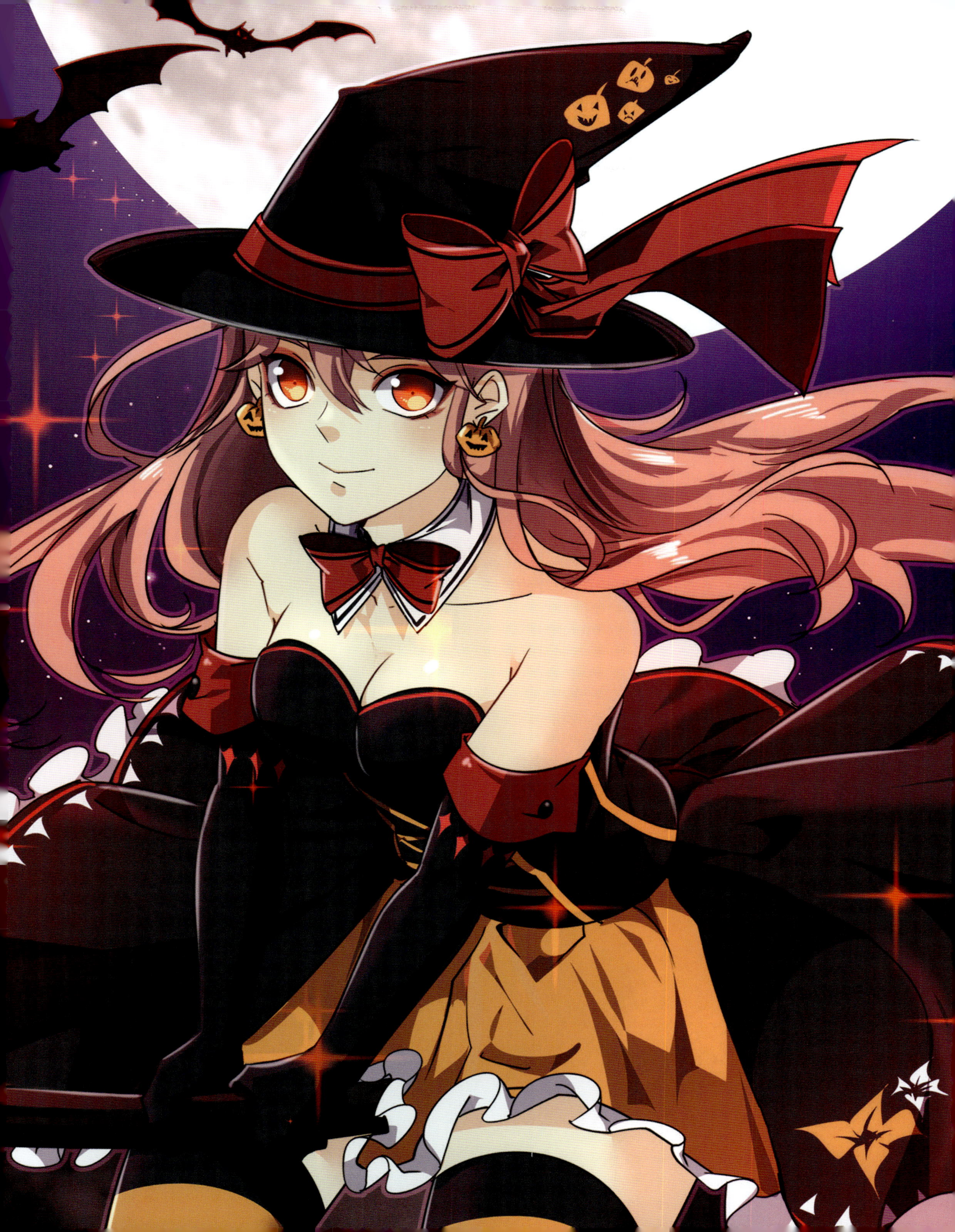

John

AGE: 18

Abilities

Aura Manipulation

Background

John is the protagonist of unOrdinary. He simply wants to be a happy, normal kid, but he's haunted by many demons; his sudden and unguided rise to power as a child makes him lose himself in the story. When his father writes him a book to help him cope with his past mistakes—titled *Unordinary*, mirroring the name of the series—John ends up spending most of his time trying to rediscover and rebuild himself.

He is an average-looking teen with charcoal black hair and light brown eyes that transform to a fiery orange glow when using his powers. He is relatively tall with an athletic build.

COLOR PALETTE

HAIR HIGHLIGHT	HAIR MIDTONE	HAIR UNDERTONE	EYE HIGHLIGHT	EYE MIDTONE
#7A7879	#323031	#1C1A1D	#FCECB0	#B1A386

Appearance

John has three distinct story arcs, each represented by his hairstyle at the time.

John, the Powerless

Hiding his powers, John wore his hair gelled down tightly to frame the sides of face, save for a single lock falling in the middle of his forehead. This deliberately conservative look could be interpreted as symbolizing John's self-control during this time.

John, Revealed

John's formerly meticulously styled hair becomes disheveled and wild. He reached his breaking point and unleashes the devastating ability of Aura Manipulation: copying the abilities of others and then amplifying their own power against them. He becomes increasingly more violent and cruel during this part of the story.

John, Balanced

John's current hair is the intersection of both of his previous eras: it's styled and contained in the back but loose in the front.

Seraphina

AGE: 18

Abilities

Time Manipulation

Background

Seraphina is a girl from a prestigious family who is gifted with extraordinary strength and ability. Prior to befriending John, she concentrated on maintaining a perfect image to fulfill the wishes and expectations of her family and others. As the highly revered Queen of Wellston, she acted indifferently toward those weaker than herself, all the while secretly envying them for being free of the burden of status and hierarchy. Seraphina is calm, cool, and hard to rattle, a result of most things in life coming easy to her.

After Seraphina and John become friends, she begins to live true to herself, allowing her crisp school uniform to wrinkle, and (literally) letting her hair down. Around this time, Seraphina drops her Queen title and is recognized by the rest of the school as the unofficial Ace. Influenced both by John and the mysterious book *Unordinary*, Seraphina begins intervening on behalf of the bullied, and she realizes the true extent of injustice in the world.

COLOR PALETTE

HAIR HIGHLIGHT	HAIR MIDTONE	HAIR UNDERTONE	EYE HIGHLIGHT	EYE MIDTONE
#E0F8A2	#CB81A4	#6E405D	#E0FAF9	#9BD1E9

Appearance

Seraphina is teenage girl with striking magenta hair and bangs. She has blue eyes that glow when using her time-control abilities. Her appearance can be categorized into two distinct eras.

Queen of Wellston (Pre-John)

Before the series begins. Seraphina wears her school uniform exactly as it's intended to be worn: crisp white shirt tucked into her skirt, and neat black tie over gray sweater vest. She wore her long magenta hair in a high, straight ponytail behind her signature bangs.

Laid-back (Post-John)

During the storyline of unOrdinary, Seraphina's hair is cut very short to just below the chin, with yellow-green highlights fading up from the tips of her bangs. She is commonly seen wearing hair extensions that are also highlighted, with her hair loose and free. Her school uniform is untucked, occasionally wrinkled, and she is sometimes seen wearing her green Wellston jacket off-the-shoulder. Outside of Wellston, she wears casual, mostly unisex clothing, but she likes to show her bare shoulders.

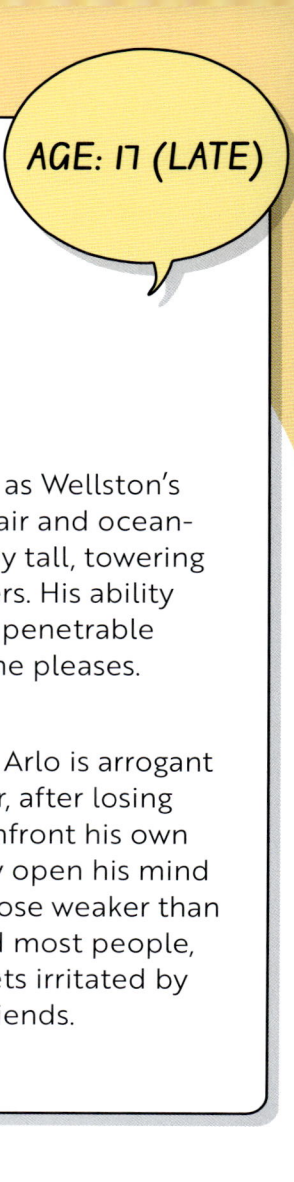

Arlo

AGE: 17 (LATE)

Abilities

Barrier

Background

Arlo begins the series as Wellston's King. He has blonde hair and ocean-blue eyes, and he is very tall, towering over most other characters. His ability allows him to create an impenetrable protective field wherever he pleases.

At the start of unOrdinary, Arlo is arrogant and domineering. However, after losing to John, he is forced to confront his own pride, and begins to slowly open his mind to the idea of caring for those weaker than himself. He is smug around most people, but he is protective and gets irritated by the choices made by his friends.

HAIR HIGHLIGHT #FCFFF6

HAIR MIDTONE #FEEFAA

HAIR UNDERTONE #C3A688

EYE HIGHLIGHT #D5FCF9

EYE MIDTONE #9BD9E8

Appearance

Arlo's look has changed little throughout the story of unOrdinary. He has wavy medium-length hair and eyebrows that almost always give him a look of anger or contempt. He is known for the single errant strand that sweeps down between his eyes over his face.

Remi

AGE: 17

Abilities

Lightning

Background

Remi is the reigning Queen of Wellston, thanks to Seraphina's abdication of the throne, and she possesses the shockingly dazzling ability to control lightning. Remi's brother was killed by the group EMBER. As a result, she becomes a vigilante to seek out justice for her brother. Her nightly adventures open her eyes to the corruption and unfairness in the world around her.

Remi is positive, uplifting, and knows what she wants. She's the go-getter type but is always kind to others.

HAIR HIGHLIGHT	HAIR MIDTONE	HAIR UNDERTONE	EYE HIGHLIGHT	EYE MIDTONE
#FFD3C6	#BE8679	#966362	#FDAA82	#E66C57

Appearance

Remi has long peach-pink hair she often partially ties up in a red or blue bow. Her eyes are framed by bright rounded cat eyeliner, which is made even more striking when using her electric powers, which illuminate her eyes in an orange-red glow.

When assuming her alter-ego, the vigilante X-Rei, she wears a loose-knit cap to conceal her long hair, along with a medical face mask to cover her mouth and nose. On the mask is a doodled cat mouth and nose, giving X-Rei a permanent smirk.

Blyke

AGE: 17

Abilities

Energy Beam/Discharge

Background

Enterprising and inquisitive Isen, impulsive but well-meaning Blyke, and feisty, fair-minded Remi form an inseparable trio of friends, all of whom are allies to John and Seraphina. Over the course of the series, their actions have evolved from schoolyard shenanigans—brawling for a coveted slice of cake—to Blyke and Remi fighting as vigilantes against the powerful government organization known as EMBER. Blyke is hot-headed but a very loyal friend. A bad liar yet intuitive, he can sense when people around him are hiding secrets.

After facing off against EMBER and John, and losing to both, his confidence takes a nosedive. Soon after, he decides to become a solo vigilante to train to become stronger. In turn, he discovers how much he cares for others and accidentally makes a name for himself.

HAIR HIGHLIGHT	HAIR MIDTONE	HAIR UNDERTONE	EYE HIGHLIGHT	EYE MIDTONE
#F49092	#A84347	#62232B	#FDFFAB	#DECB7E

Appearance

Blyke is a relatively tall teenage boy with yellow eyes. His bright crimson hair is medium-length, falling just past his ears and styled in a tussled, wind-blown fashion.

As his vigilante alter-ego, Nobody, Blyke conceals his identity by wearing a gray-brown hoodie over a tight black knitted cap and a black half-balaclava covering his mouth and nose. A bombastic but well-intentioned member of the group, Blyke manifests red energy beams of various shapes and sizes from his hands, dealing surprising bursts of damage to foes.

Isen

AGE: 17

Abilities

Hunter

Background

The third member of the friend-trio alongside Remi and Blyke, Isen's abilities are not specifically combat-oriented. Instead, they are categorized under the term "hunter." His skills include tracking down targets and providing other powers of reconnaissance and support to the group. Isen likes writing and is a part of the school press team. Because he is very logical and self-preserving, Isen may be the first to back away from a risky encounter.

COLOR PALETTE

HAIR HIGHLIGHT	HAIR MIDTONE	HAIR UNDERTONE	EYE HIGHLIGHT	EYE MIDTONE
#F7F6BD	#E3B07B	#AF7F68	#FEA89B	#D9707F

Appearance

Isen is the tallest of the trio, a teenager with a layer of light-orange medium-length hair covering dark brown hair beneath. He's easy to spot thanks to the signature cowlick on the top of his head. Isen is the only member who never wears a tie with his uniform.

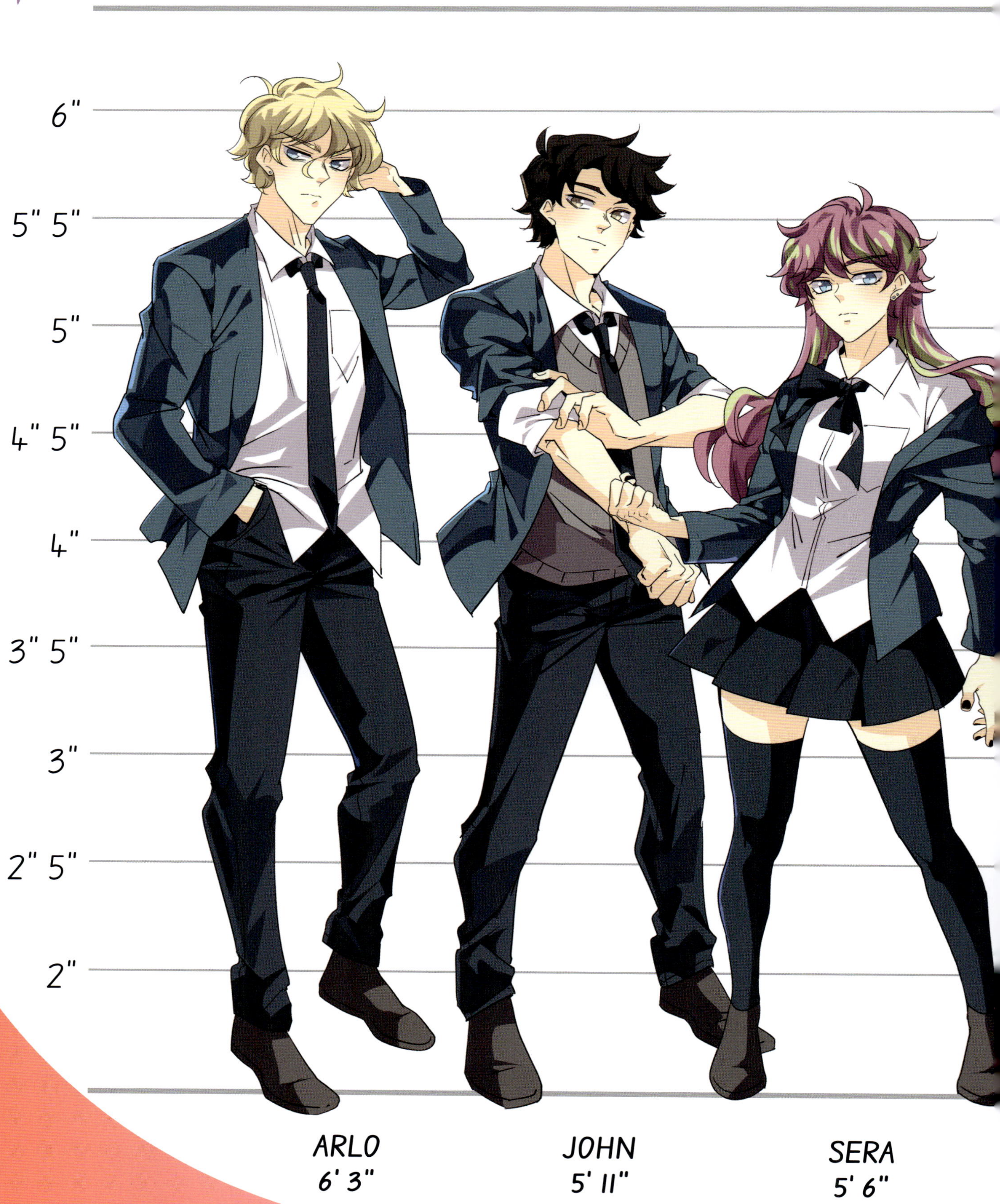
6"
5" 5"
5"
4" 5"
4"
3" 5"
3"
2" 5"
2"
ARLO
6' 3"
JOHN
5' 11"
SERA
5' 6"

Character Height Chart

When developing a cast of characters for a story, it's a good idea to map out how tall they are in relation to each other so you can keep consistency when drawing them together in various scenes.

ISEN
6'

REMI
5' 5"

BLYKE
5' 10"

Getting Started

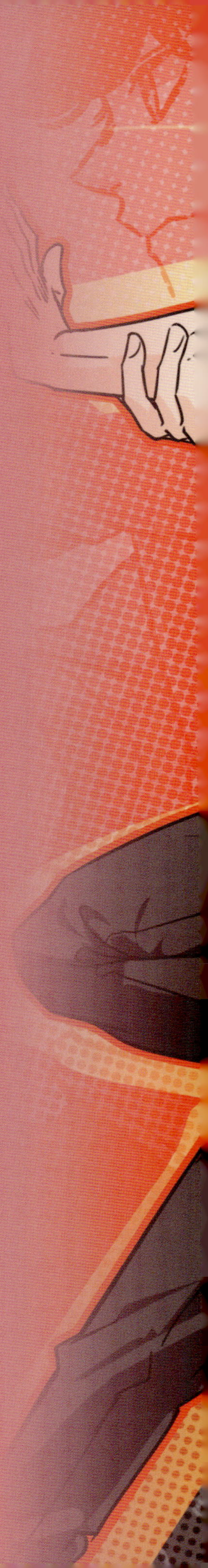

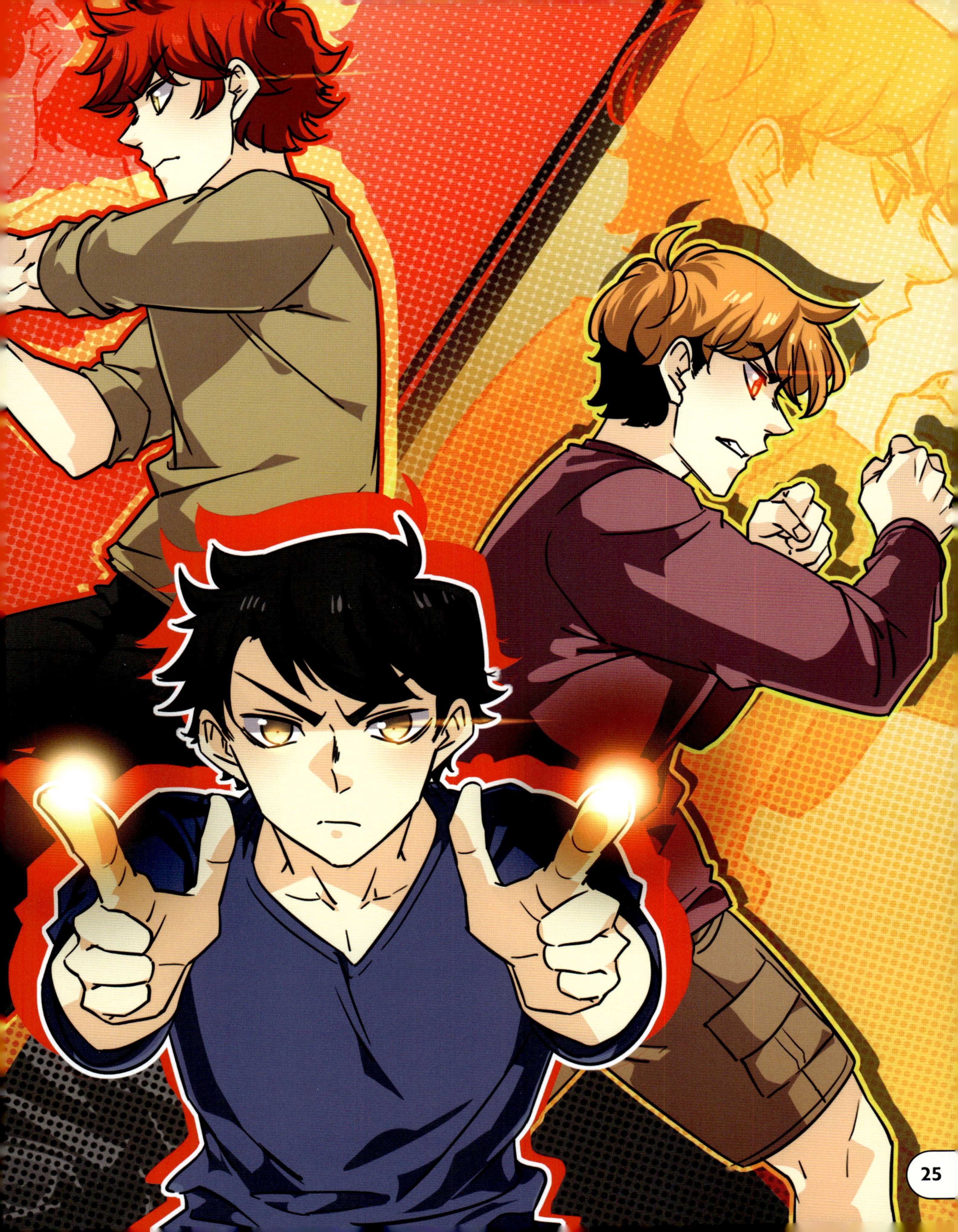

Tools & Materials

Whether you are sketching on paper or drawing digitally, there are some basic tools that will help you on your artistic journey.

Pencils

Graphite pencils come in various densities that help you achieve different shading techniques. The harder or denser the lead is, the lighter it will draw on paper. For a light shade, you can use a 2H pencil. An HB pencil will give you a medium shade, and for darker shades, you can use between 2B and 6B pencils. If you are a beginner artist, start with an HB pencil. Try different pencils and see which one works best for you.

Erasers

When cleaning up your sketches, try using a good-quality rubber or vinyl eraser. You don't want something that will smudge your artwork as you are removing guidelines. A kneaded eraser is also a great tool and is a very pliable and versatile option that won't leave any dust or residue on your paper. You can mold the eraser into any shape to erase precisely.

Pens & Inks

Fine-line markers come in different widths and are easy to use. Once you have finalized your sketches, it's a good idea to go back and finish with a clean, sharp line. Make sure to use permanent ink markers so they won't smudge when adding color or erasing pencil lines. If you want variety in your pen strokes, try using a brush pen. The more pressure you use with a brush pen, the thicker the lines. Light pressure is perfect for very fine details.

Adding Color

Colored pencils are great for adding shading and depth to your drawings. Make sure to sharpen them when using them for detail work.

Markers are perfect for adding large areas of color. Make sure to draw your strokes in quick succession to help them look smooth and blended. Add details or shading on top by letting your strokes dry first and then building up the color. Watercolor paints are a great medium for adding color to inked drawings.

Paper

A sketchbook is a great tool. Always have your sketchbook handy when developing your art practice. They come in a variety of sizes and shapes. A good mixed-media sketchbook is a great place to start. If you are using paints or markers, choose a thicker paper so the wet media doesn't bleed through.

Digital Tools

Webcomics are created digitally, so it is great to familiarize yourself with digital drawing tools. There are many different drawing apps available at a low cost; some are even free. Drawing tablets with pens can be used for digital drawing. There are many to choose from, so research and test out your options to find the right tablet for you. I use a Wacom Baboo tablet and work in Paint Tool SAI and Clip Studio Paint.

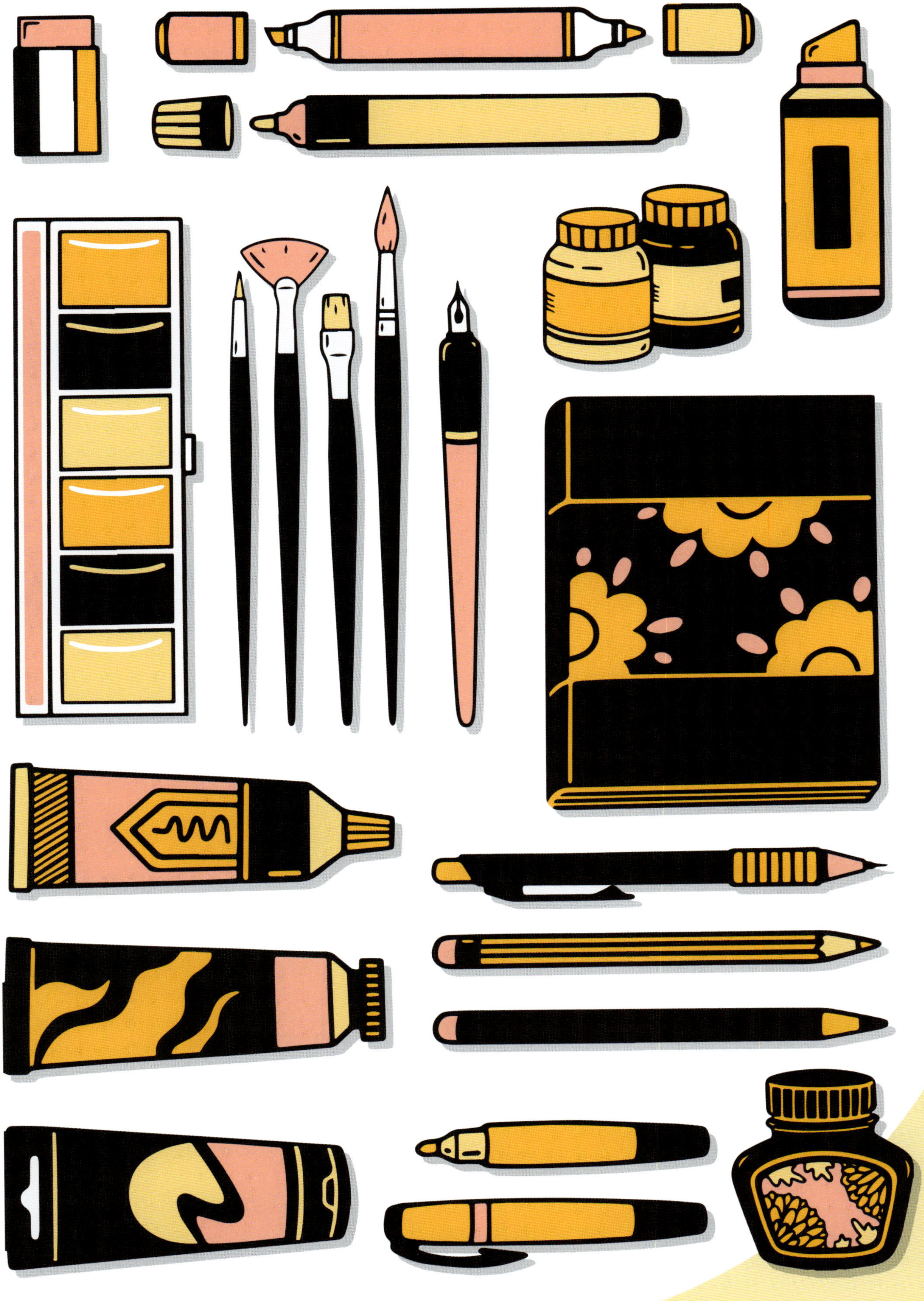

Anatomy Basics: The Head

It's important to have a solid grasp of the basics when drawing characters. One of the easiest ways to learn how to draw a three-dimensional figure on a two-dimensional surface is to understand the fundamentals of basic human anatomy.

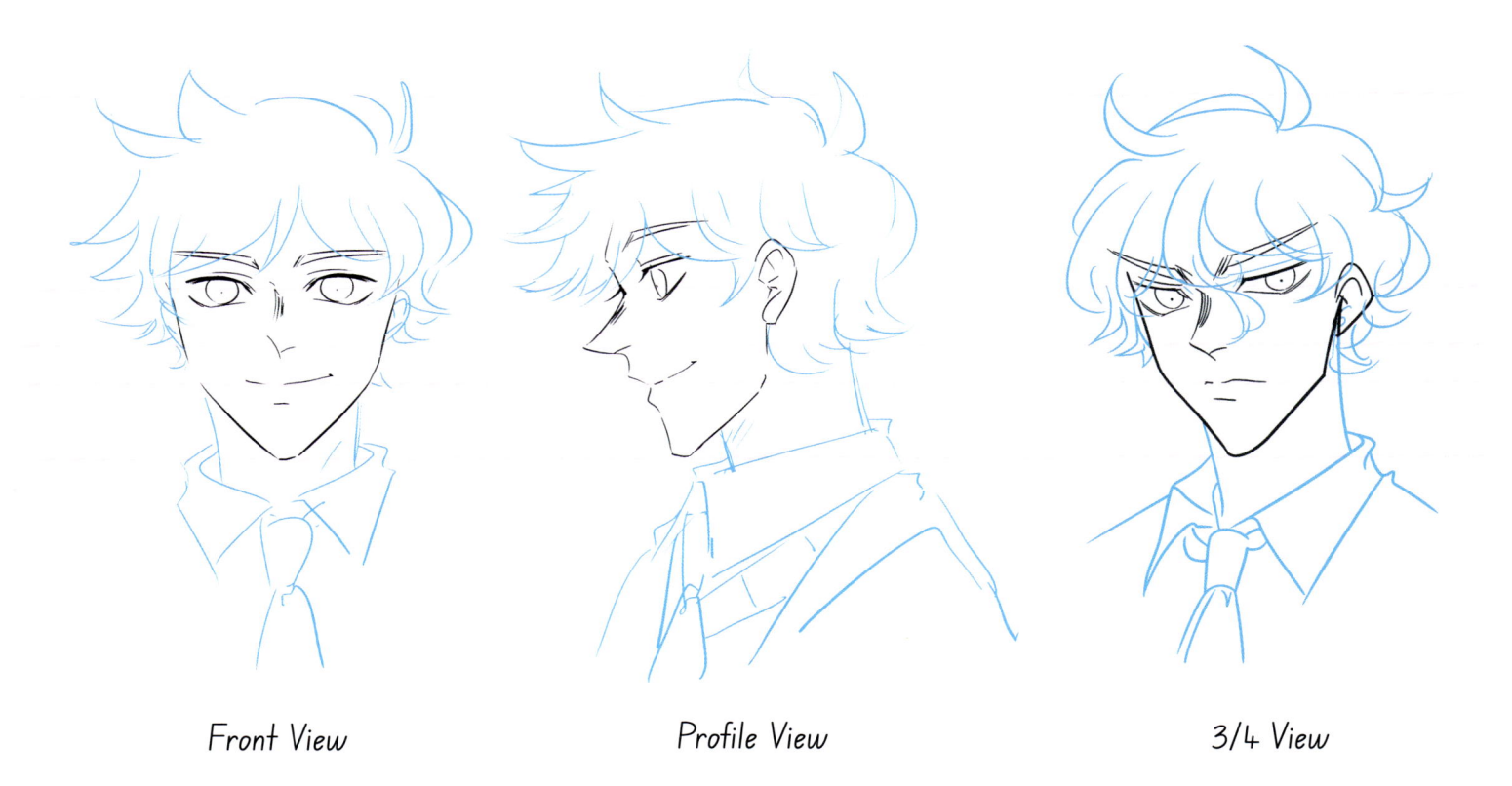

Front View   Profile View   3/4 View

When drawing faces, you'll generally begin with a rough sketch of the head. Sometimes it's helpful to begin with a circle, or oval, and guidelines to indicate where to add the features. From there, you can begin roughing in the facial features and developing the shape of the face. The upper eyelids generally align with the top of the ear; the bridge of the nose is usually dead center between the eye pupils when the head is facing forward.

Start by learning to draw the head and face in a front-facing position. Once you've mastered using guidelines for placing the features, you can use the same method to draw the head at different angles, such as three-quarter (3/4) and profile views.

There are three basic views of the face: the front view, the three-quarter view, and the side view. When the head is kept level, the horizontal guidelines stay the same. When the chin tilts up or down, the horizontal guidelines curve with the form of the head.

FRONT VIEW

3/4 VIEW

PROFILE VIEW

Expressions

Expressions are important because they help convey a character's mood and motivation while also contributing to the action of each scene.

CUTE

INTENSE

SAD

ANNOYED

HAPPY

INDIFFERENT

Most expressions can be conveyed through the eyes and the mouth. Wide eyes can express things like surprise, excitement, and shock. Open mouths can be shaped downward to convey alarm or anger, while upward-shaped mouths communicate excitement and joy.

Narrowed eyes indicate laid-back mood.

Tight grip shows tense posture.

Squared shoulders show the character is alert and ready for action.

When drawing expressions, be sure to match the emotion with the corresponding body language.

Relaxed eyes convey mood.

Backward cap and bubble gum add fun and interest.

Soft shoulders, leaning posture, and hands in pockets show the character's laid back mood.

Once you have a character's facial proportions down, it's fairly simple to adjust the expression. Start with a neutral face like the one shown. Then play around with the eyes, eyebrows, and mouth to create different looks.

Anatomy Basics: The Body

Body height is generally measured in head size, which means each section of the body is roughly the same size as the head. Most adult bodies are between six and eight heads tall; however, think of these proportions as rough guidelines. Your characters' proportions might vary depending on their unique qualities.

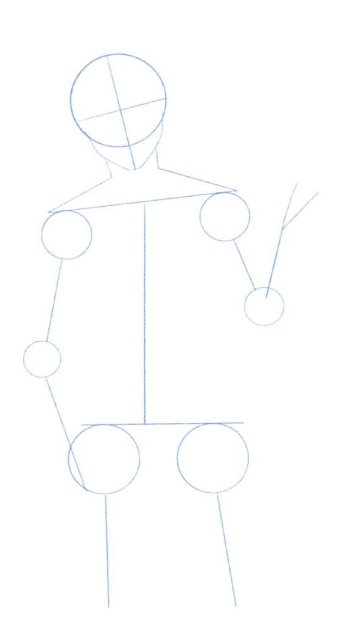

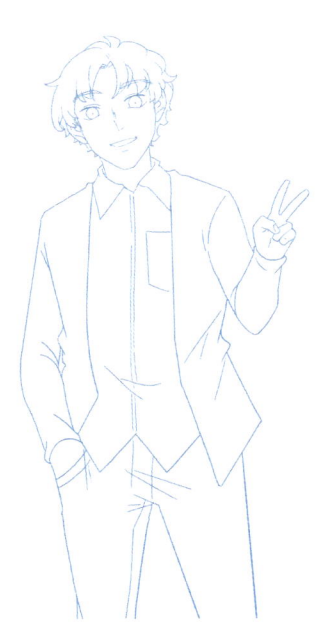

You can also divide the body in half from the top of the head to the groin and from the groin to the bottom of the feet.

Imagine one vertical line that divides the body in half. This line represents the spine. Add horizontal lines for each body segment. This will help to get the proportions correct.

When the body is facing forward, it's easy to align it to horizontal and vertical axis lines. When the body moves, however, the axis lines also move. Notice the natural contours of the body when the chest, neck, face, and pelvis are facing other directions. Becoming familiar with the body's movements will help your character poses look natural.

Neck rotated

Slight curve in the spine

Torso turned

Arms folded

The wrist is typically at the same level as the hips. Elbows are either at the same level as, or a little higher than, the waist.

Slight bend in the knees

Foot position turned

Still and Dynamic Poses

In webcomics, action in a scene is demonstrated through a character's pose and movements as well as the setting, background, and other details. Sometimes the pose is still, or static, meaning the character isn't moving much. Sometimes the pose is dynamic, meaning the character is in motion.

Still Pose

Details can show character movement concurrent with a static pose. Here, John is drinking a mango boba, but his overall posture is still.

Dynamic Pose

Adding highlights, shading, and motion lines at the color stage can help communicate a body in motion.

This scene conveys both static and dynamic action. The tension between the two characters is communicated through their tightened facial expressions, clenched fists, and firm grips. It's a brief moment of tense stillness and we can anticipate the dynamic action to come in the next scene.

Chibi Heads and Bodies

Chibi characters are usually between two and three heads tall. It doesn't matter whether heads and bodies are full size or chibi size; the process for drawing them is the same. Start with your head-to-body ratio to draw your chibi character in correct proportion. Add guidelines to help place features, and rough in the details of the pose.

Chibi movements follow the same basic principles of average-sized figures in that the horizontal axis, or spine, twists and turns with their bodies.

Chibi characters might have slightly bigger heads than average-sized characters. Conversely, their arms, hands, legs, and feet might be disproportionally small. It's these exaggerated characteristics that give chibis their cute factor.

BLAH BLAH

Sometimes less is more when drawing chibis. You can simplify the details in their faces, limbs, and bodies without sacrificing the quality of the drawing. It's one of the fun parts about drawing chibis. You can take more artistic liberties with the characters because they are meant to be exaggerated.

Character Sheets

Creating character sheets is a great way to work out who your character is. Character sheets are like the first draft in writing, and you can create as many as you need to work out everything about your characters, from their physical features and personality traits to their color palettes. They are also helpful for taking notes and documenting the evolution of your characters' styles as they change over the course of your webcomic series. Here are some of my character sheets.

John

Clothing Style (casual, generally dark)

Sample Character Sheet

Colors

Hairstyles

Gelled/slicked (powerless hairstyle)

Chaotic hairstyle

Side part (powerless hairstyle)

He is the only person that
wears his vest from the main cast.

Spiky hair in front

Rounded hair
in back

Rounded
eyes

Sharper chin

Seraphina

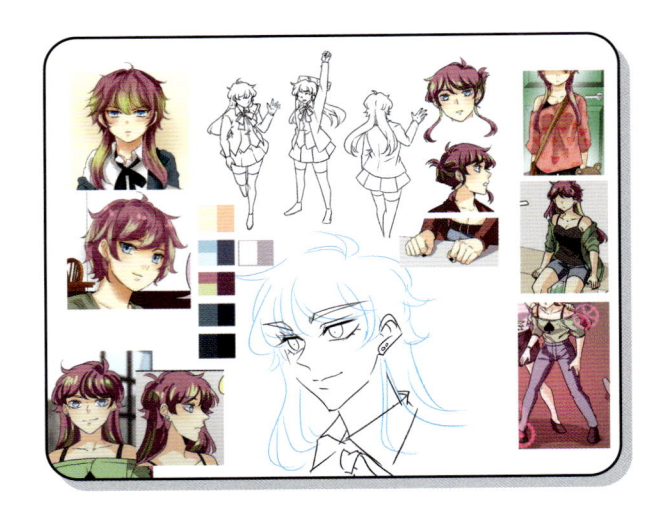

Previous Style (clothing and hair)

Jacket dropping

Colors

Alternate Hairstyle (no extensions)

Clothing Style (recent)

Black Nail Polish

Recent Style

Alternate Hairstyle (hair clip)

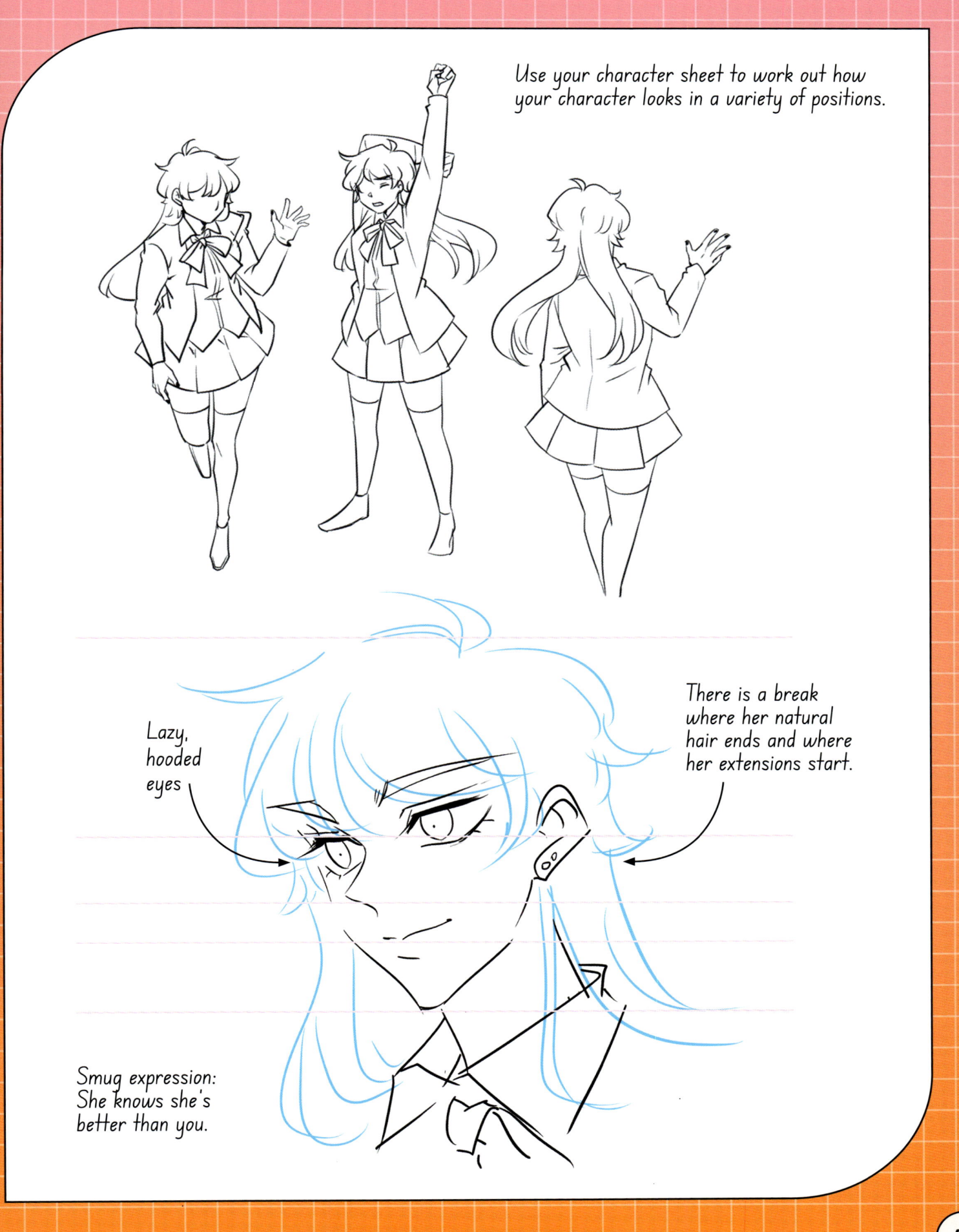

Use your character sheet to work out how your character looks in a variety of positions.

There is a break where her natural hair ends and where her extensions start.

Lazy, hooded eyes

Smug expression: She knows she's better than you.

Arlo

Previous Style (clothing and hair)

Colors

Clothing Style (formal and preppy)

Current Style (clothing and hair)

Rough sketches are helpful for creating storyboards for your webcomic. You can work out character placements and positions without rendering complete drawings.

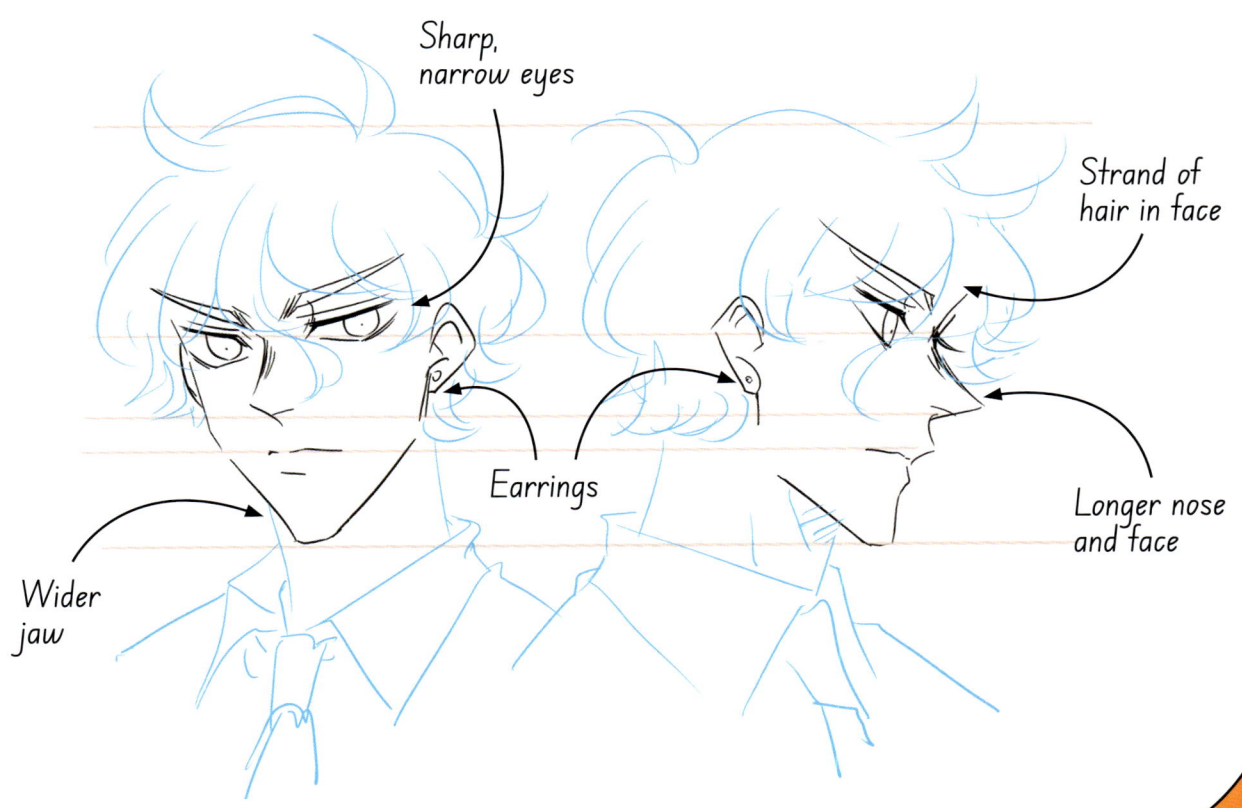

Sharp, narrow eyes

Strand of hair in face

Earrings

Longer nose and face

Wider jaw

Remi

Previous Style (clothing and hair)

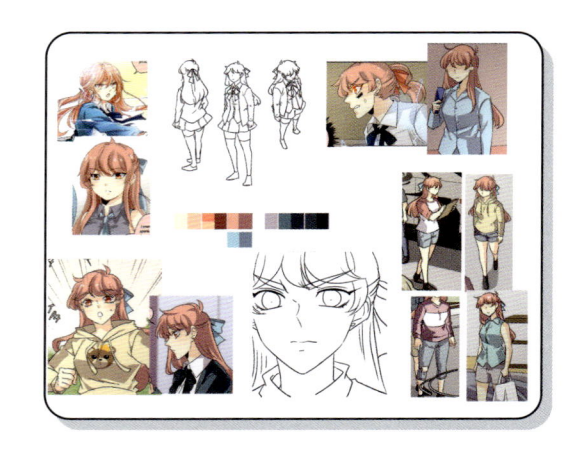

Colors

Clothing Style

Current Style (clothing and hair)

Alternate Hairstyles

44

Rounded, innocent eyes

Cat eyeliner

Rounded face

When creating character sheets, you may choose to focus on perfecting specific elements instead of rendering completed illustrations. My sketch here is incomplete because I am working on my stroke precision.

Blyke

Colors

Blyke looks similar to John.

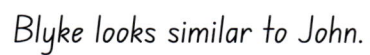

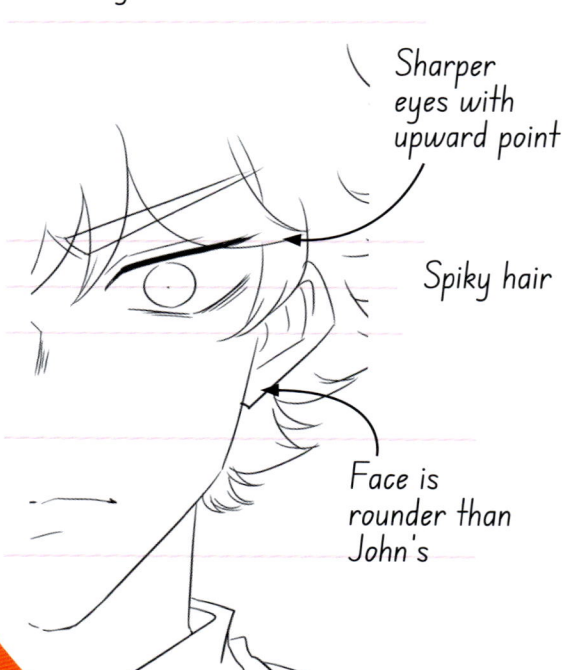

Sharper eyes with upward point

Spiky hair

Face is rounder than John's

Previous Style

Current Style

Isen

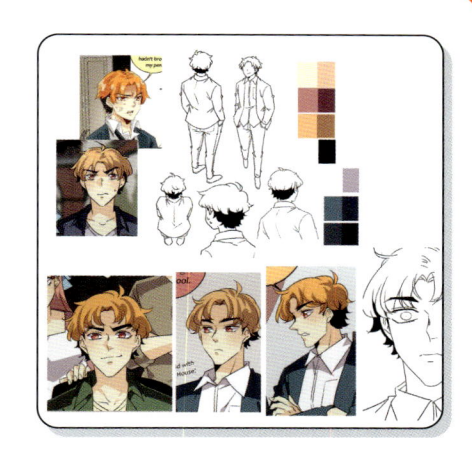

Colors

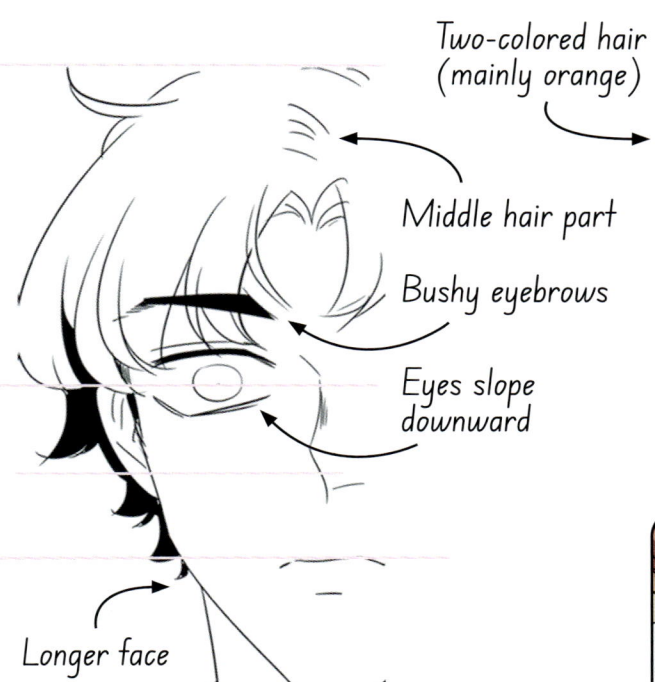

Two-colored hair
(mainly orange)

Middle hair part

Bushy eyebrows

Eyes slope
downward

Longer face

Previous Style

Current Style

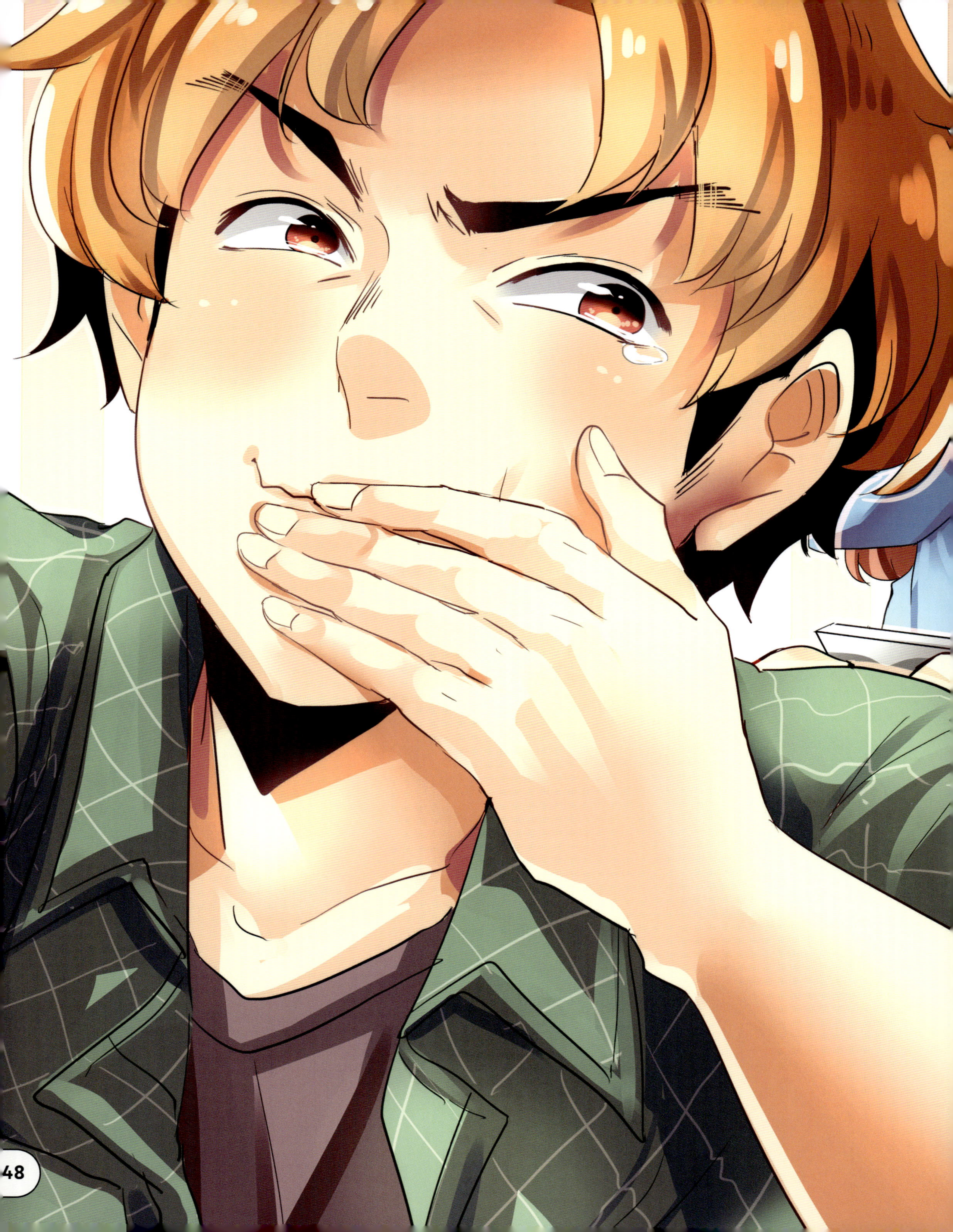

Drawing
Step by Step

Learn to draw your favorite characters from unOrdinary.

John: Head (3/4 View)

Begin with a circle. Add a vertical guideline marking the direction of the head and the face. Add horizontal guidelines to help determine where to place the features. Begin to shape the chin and rough in the details. Don't get discouraged if your drawing doesn't turn out "perfect" the first time. Drawing takes practice. Simply follow the steps and, in time, your skills will improve.

5

When you are satisfied with your drawing, erase any old sketch lines and add color using the tools of your choice.

6

John has a triangular-shaped face with a strong, angular jawline. His features are sharp and pointy.

John: Full Body (3/4 View)

Begin with a circle for the head and guidelines for the facial features. Add vertical and horizontal axis lines and circles to denote the joints, such as the shoulders, elbows, and knees. Continue to fill in the form following the steps.

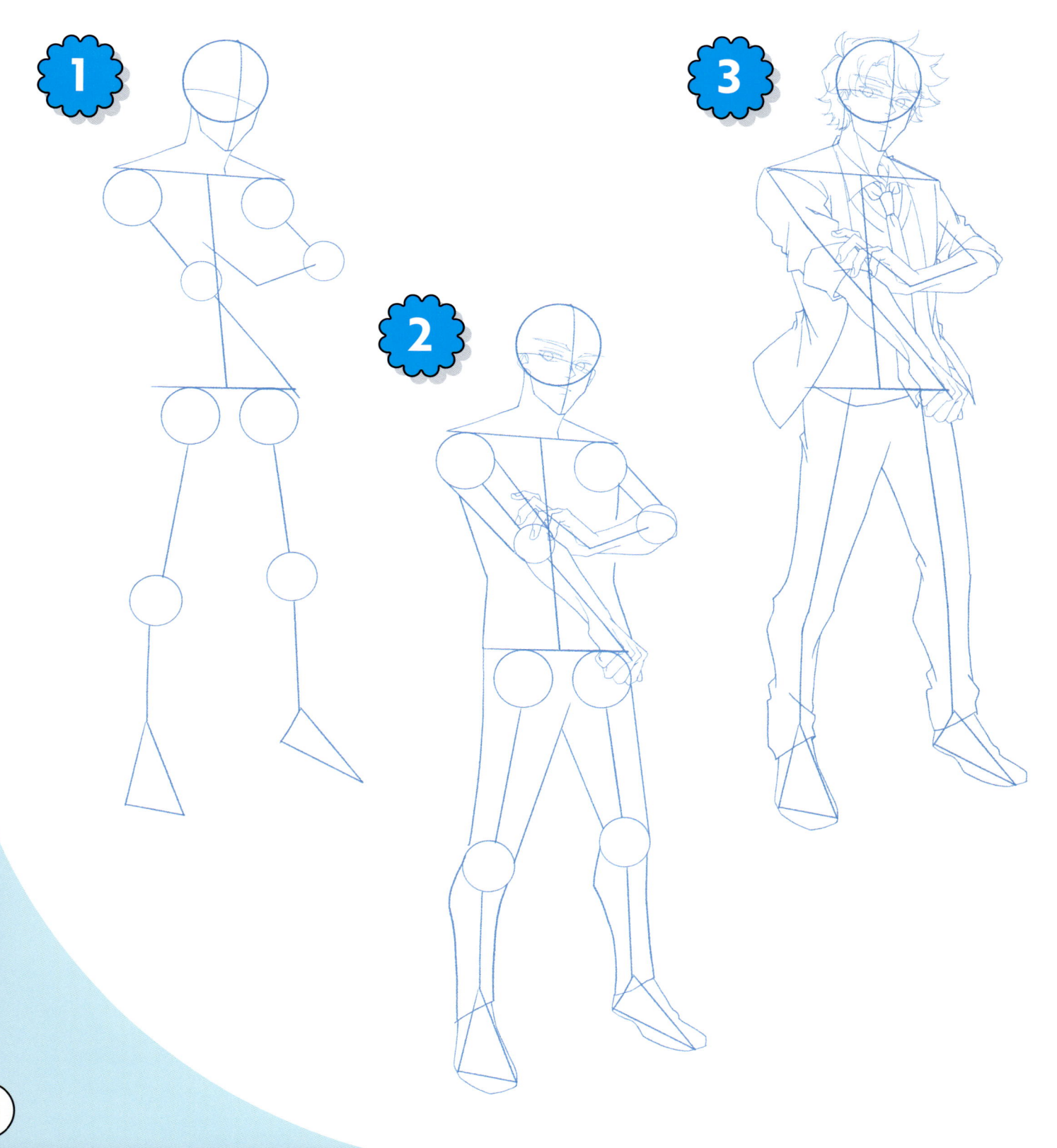

4

When you are satisfied with your drawing, erase any old sketch lines and add color using the tools of your choice.

5

Notice how John's gaze is aimed slightly further to the right than the direction of his head. Pay attention to these little details to help your drawings feel polished and professional.

John: Action Pose

Notice how the body moves and contorts with the action of this pose. Simply start with a circle, facial guidelines, and vertical and horizontal axis lines. Then, denote the joints with circles. Follow the steps to fill in the details.

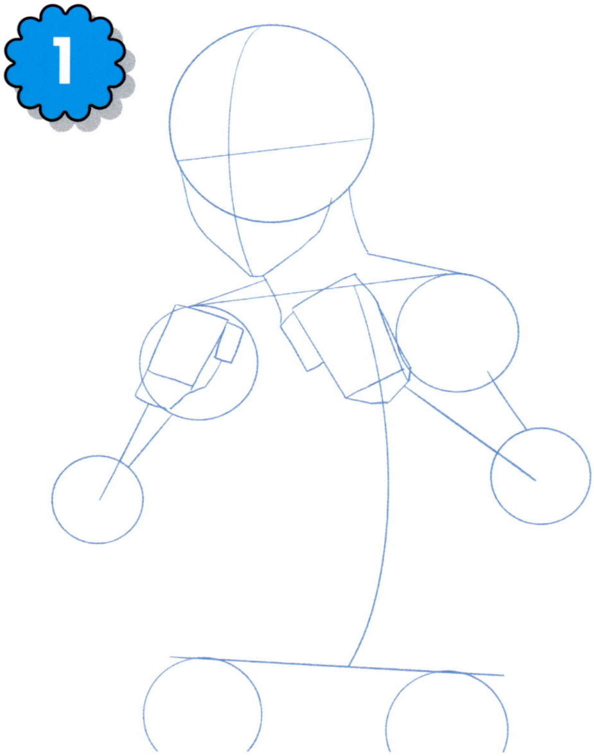
1

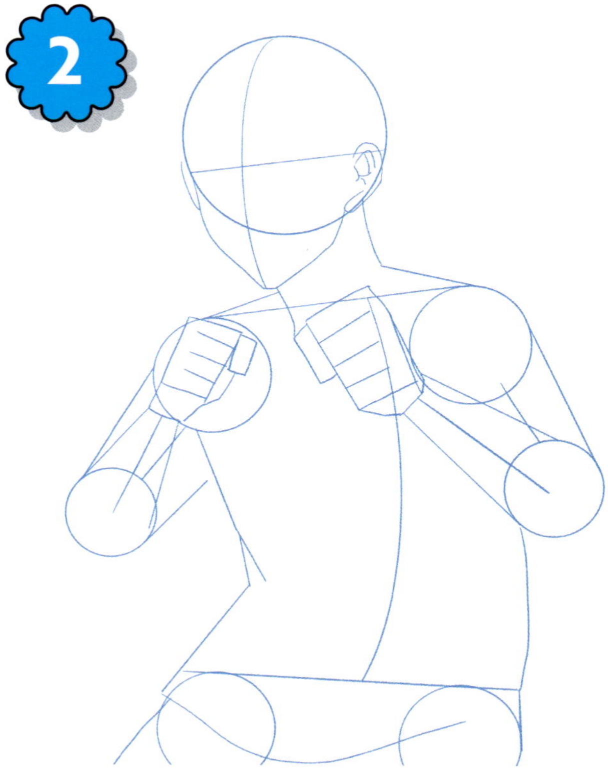
2

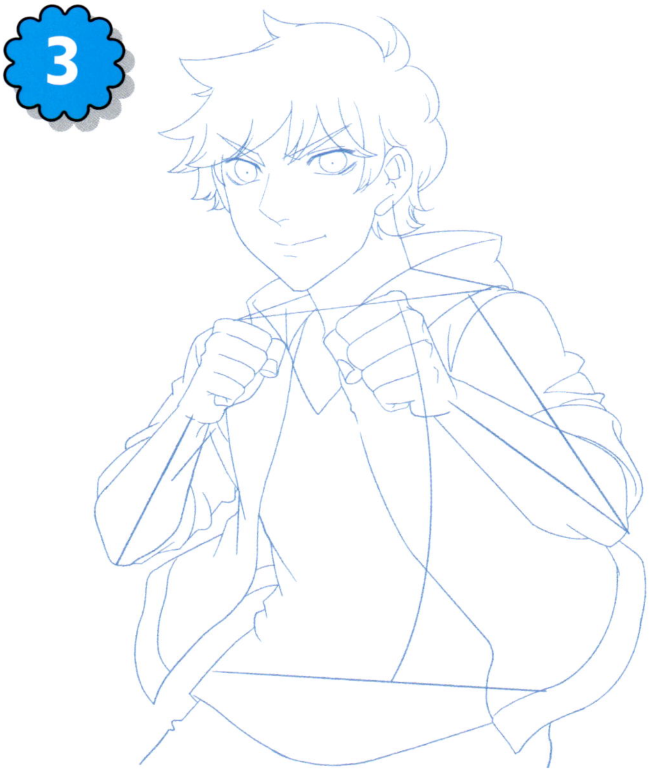
3

4

When you are satisfied with your drawing, erase any old sketch lines and add color using the tools of your choice.

5

Adding one or two shades of red to John's bandaged knuckles adds interest to this action pose.

Seraphina: Head (Front View)

Begin with a circle. Add a vertical guideline marking the forward direction of the head and the face. Add horizontal guidelines to help determine where to place the features. Shape the chin and rough in the details.

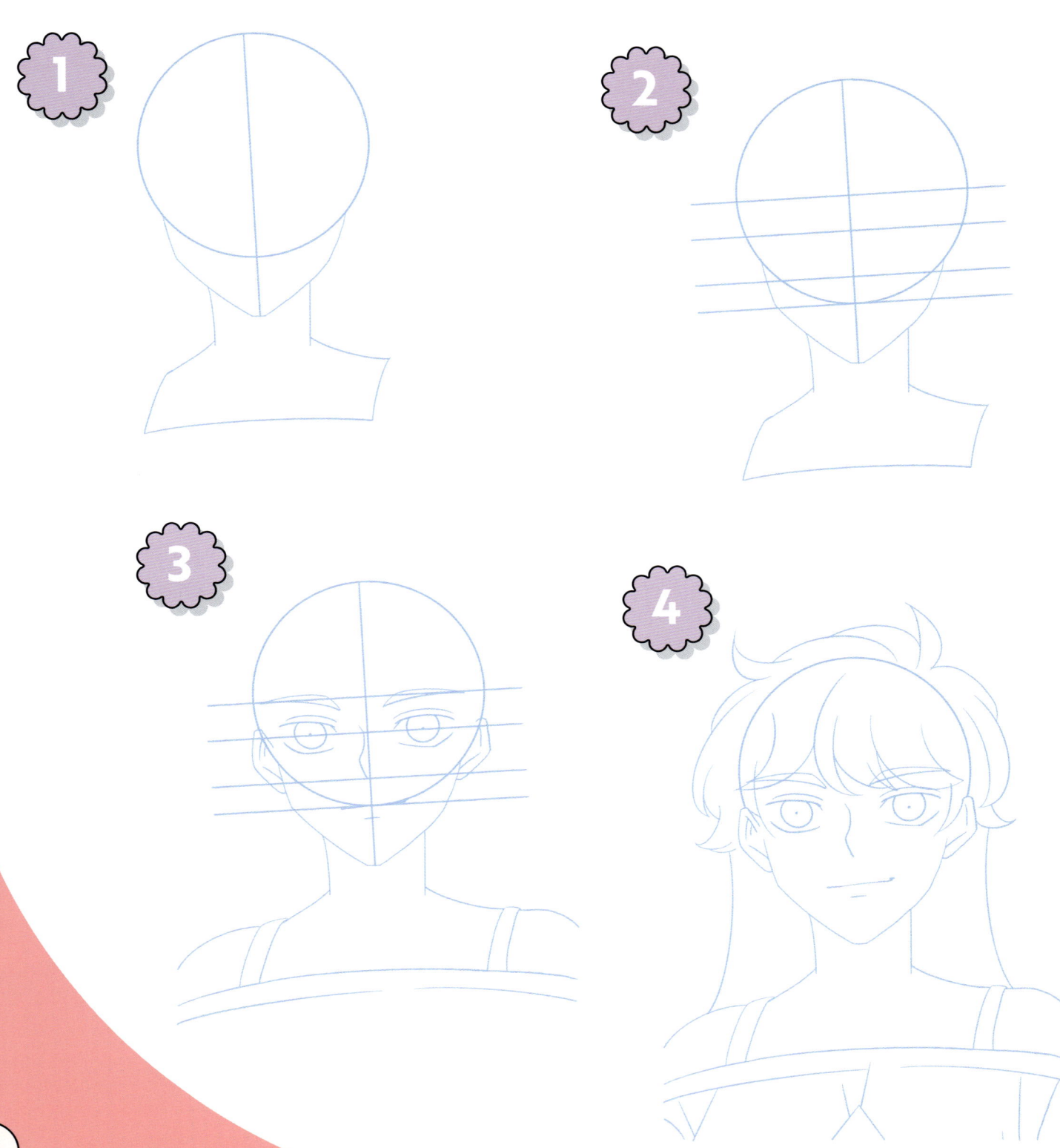

5

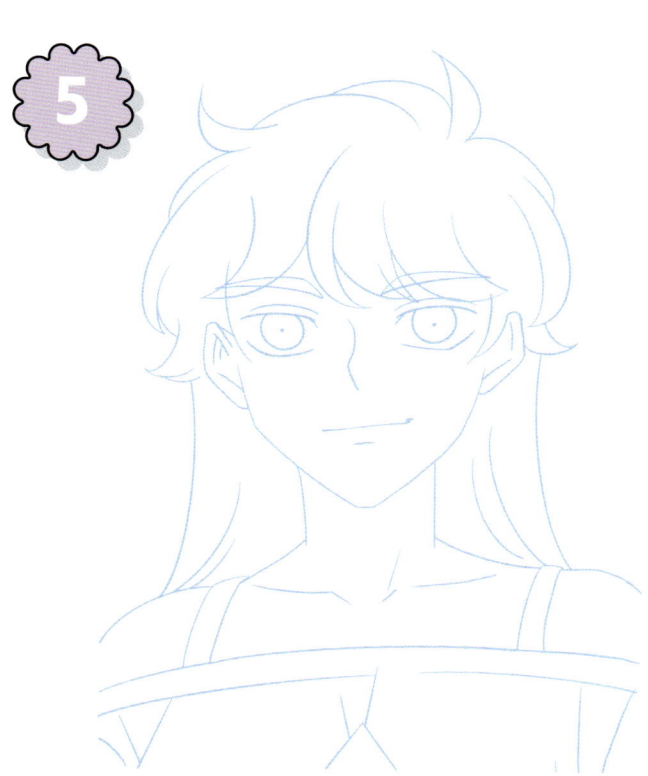

When you are satisfied with your drawing, erase any old sketch lines and add color using the tools of your choice.

6

Don't forget to add Seraphina's signature highlights in her bangs and extensions.

Seraphina: Full Body (3/4 View)

Start with a circle for the head and guidelines for the face. Add vertical and horizontal axis lines; then denote the joints with circles and the feet with triangles. Follow the steps to fill in the details.

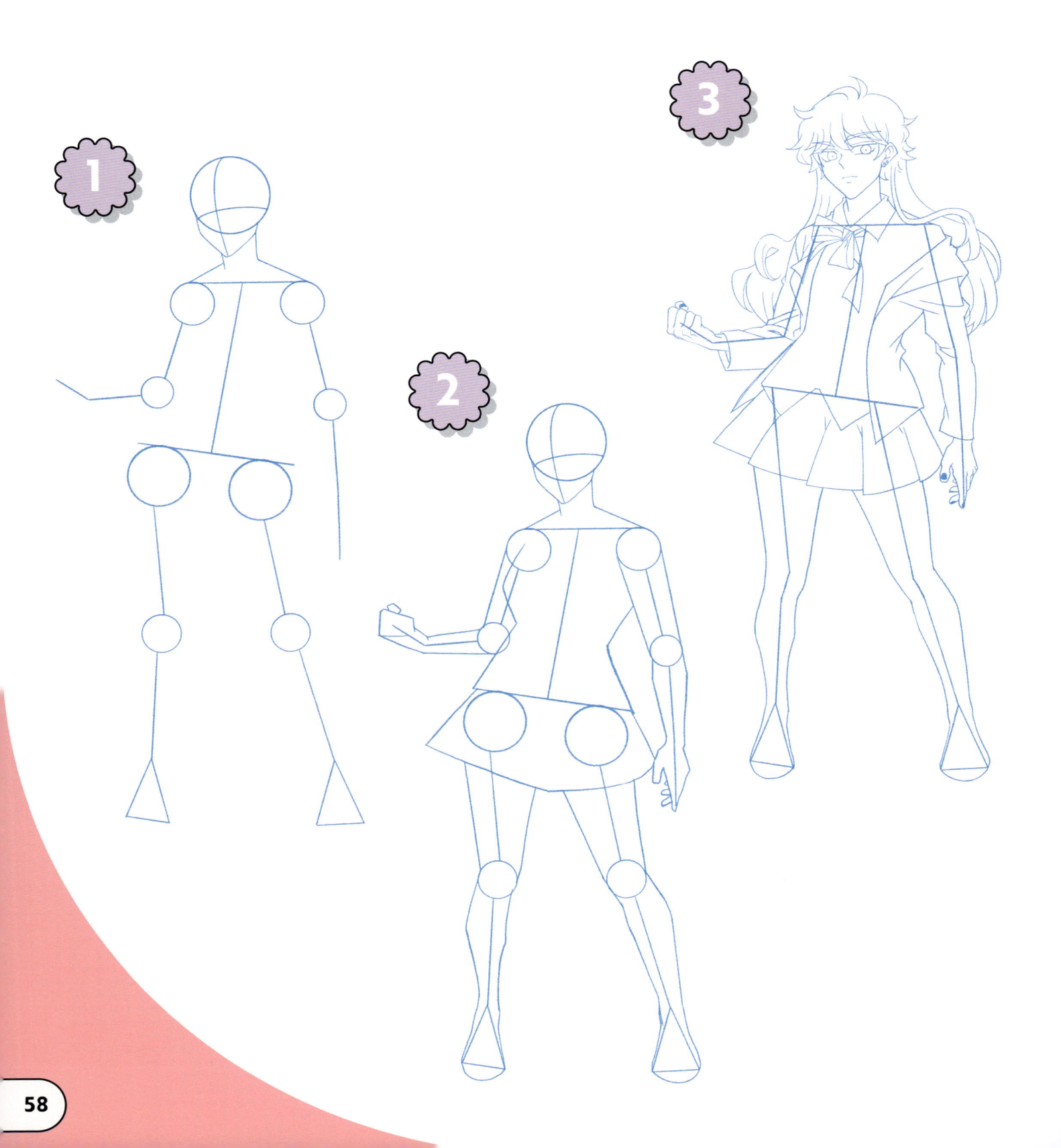

4

When you are satisfied with your drawing, erase any old sketch lines and add color using the tools of your choice.

5

Notice how the shading in Sera's pleated skirt gives it a sense of motion. As though she's just slightly moved her hips when she formed a fist. Is her pose still or dynamic?

Seraphina: Still Pose

Although she's holding a phone, Seraphina's movement is paused and she is not in motion. This is considered a static pose. However, notice how her earrings appear to sway, suggesting she's just turned her head. Begin this pose with a circle and guidelines for the head and the face. Add axis lines and circles for the joints. Then rough in the details.

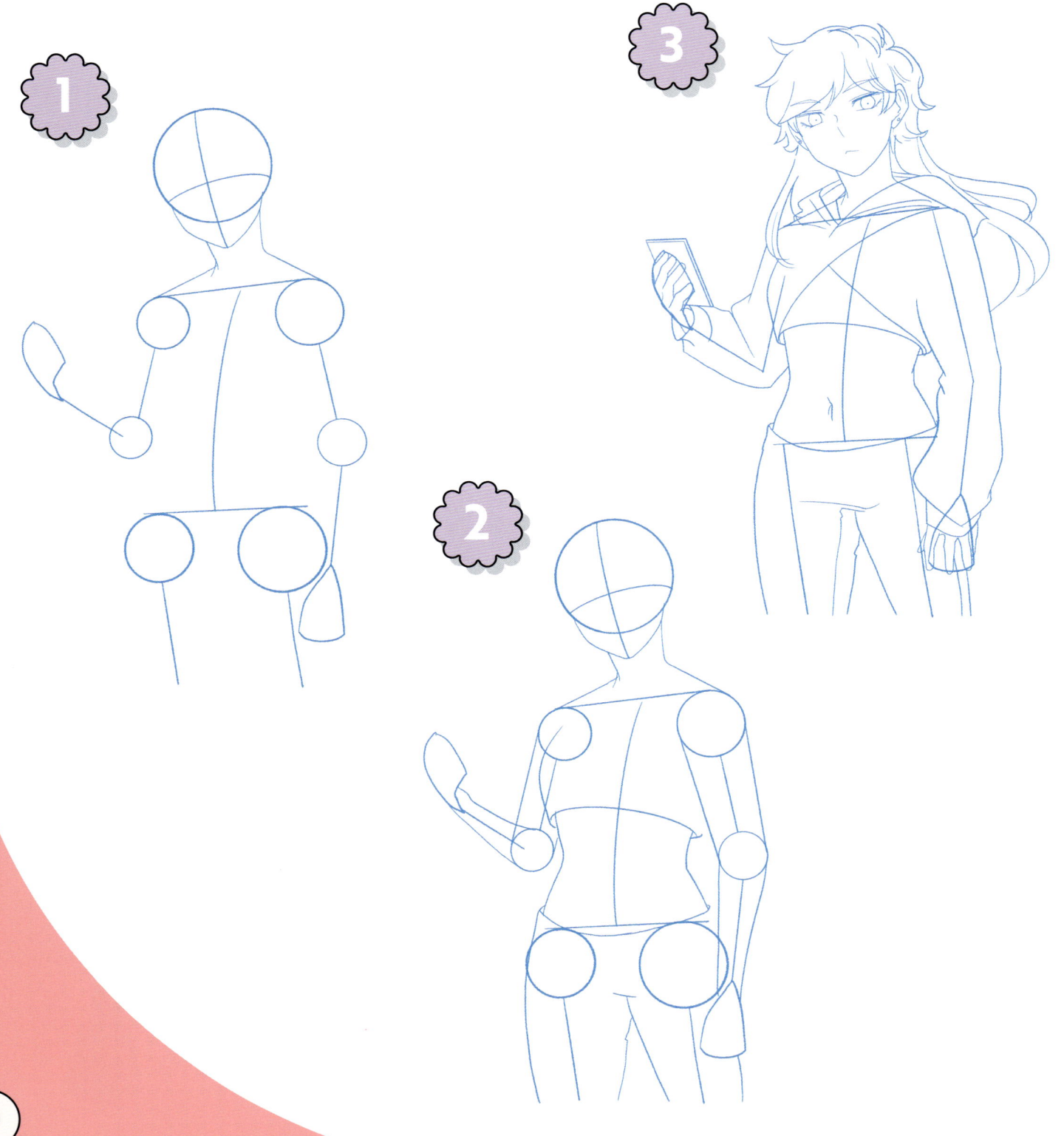

4

5

When you are satisfied with your drawing, erase any old sketch lines and add color using the tools of your choice.

Props, accessories, and clothes allow you to communicate who your character is through your drawing.

John & Seraphina: Group Pose

Group poses can be challenging especially if the characters are in radically different positions, like in this one with John, who is looking up, and Seraphina, who is looking down. Start the same way as with the other drawings by sketching in circles for the heads and guidelines for the bodies. Take your time as you rough in the details.

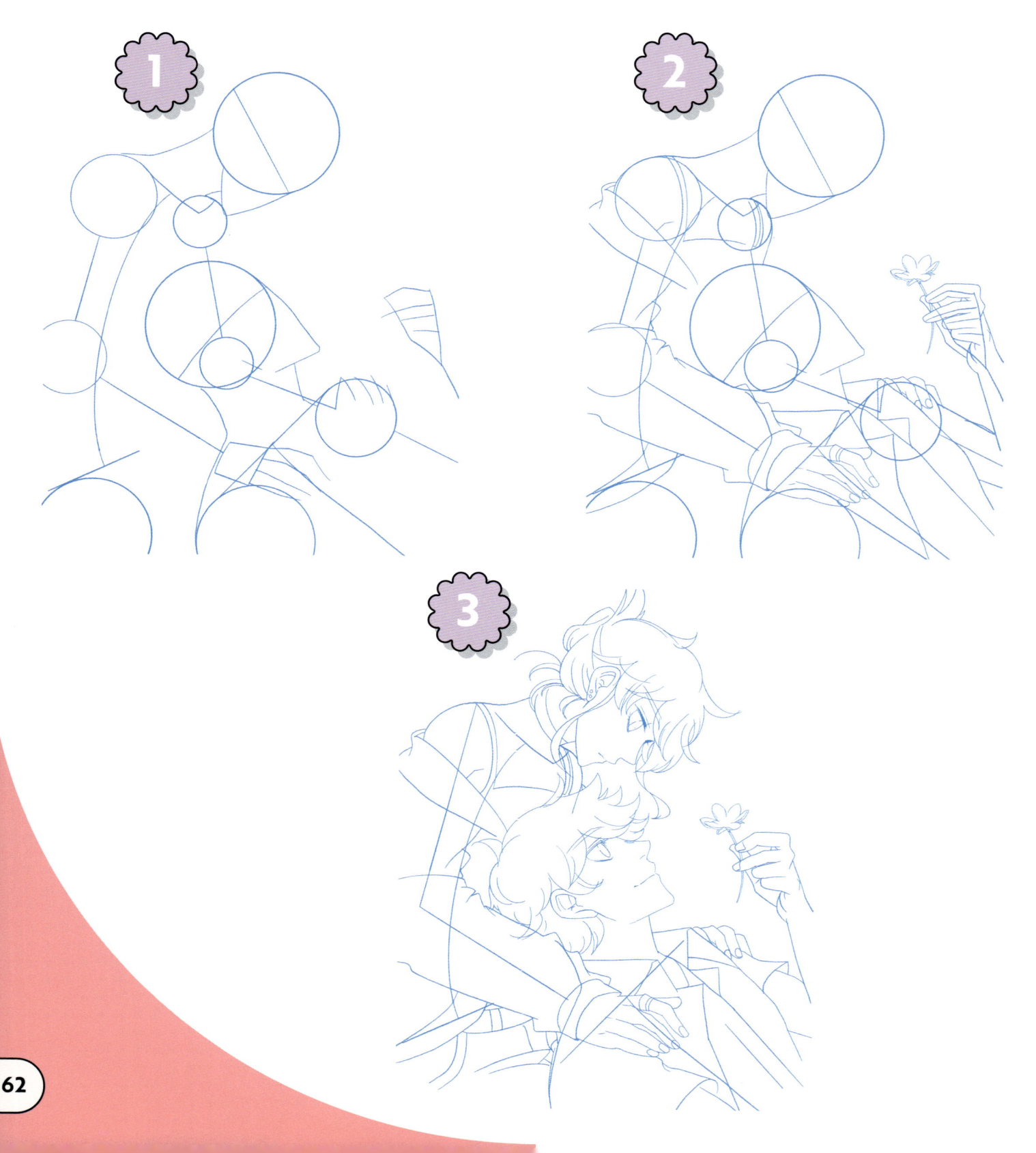

When you are satisfied with your drawing, erase any old sketch lines and add color using the tools of your choice.

4

5

Harmonizing color palettes can help communicate the mood and atmosphere in a scene, whether it's relaxed, as shown here, or tense.

Arlo: Head (Front View)

Begin with a circle. Add a vertical guideline marking the forward direction of the head and the face. Add horizontal guidelines to help determine where to place the features. Rough in the shape of the chin and complete the details.

5

When you are satisfied with your drawing, erase any old sketch lines and add color using the tools of your choice.

6

Like John, Arlo has an angular jaw and strong, geometrical features. Notice how his hair is a bit messy.

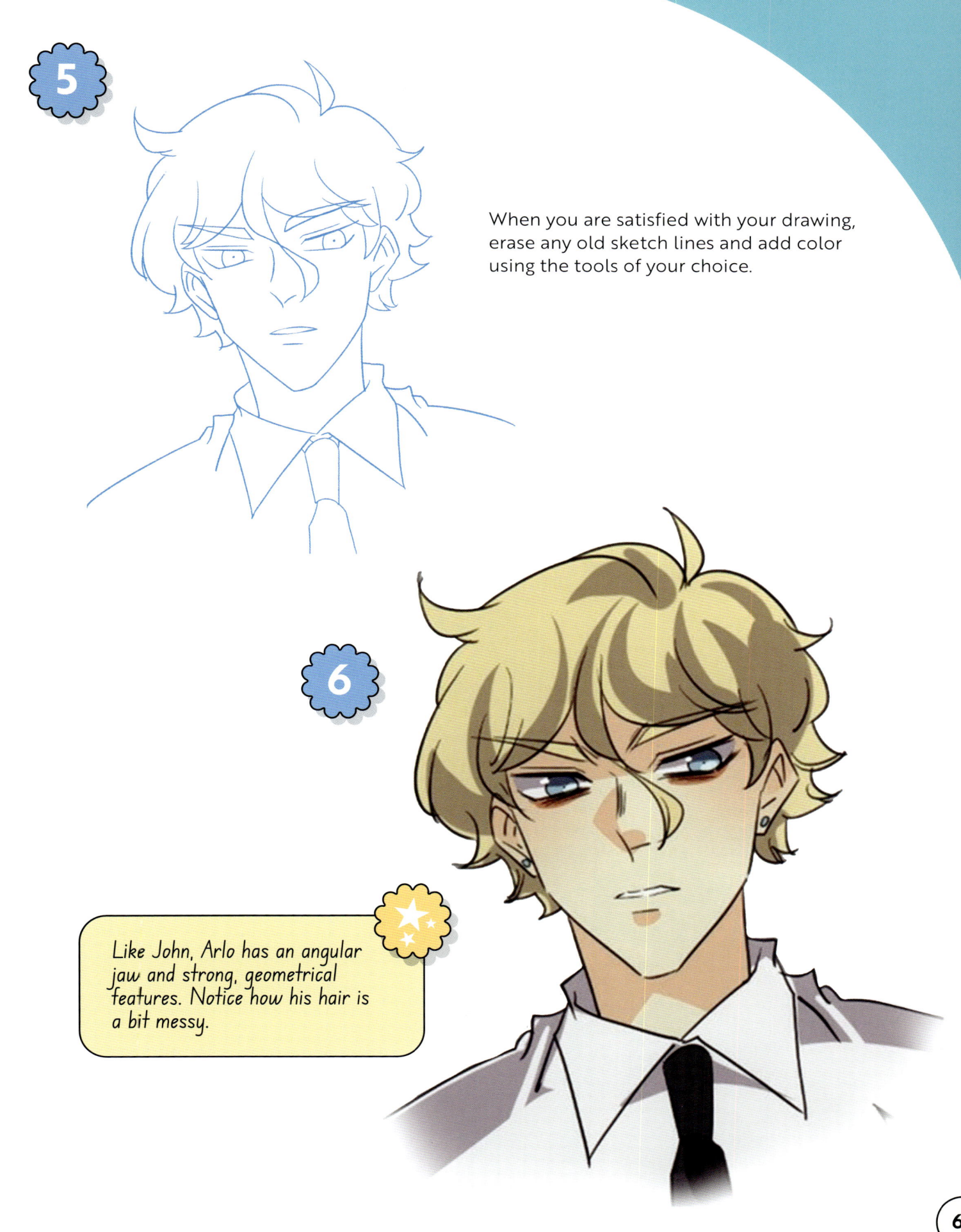

Arlo: Full Body (3/4 View)

Start with a circle for the head and guidelines for the face. Add vertical and horizontal axis lines; then denote the joints with circles and the feet with triangles. Follow the steps to fill in the details.

4

When you are satisfied with your drawing, erase any old sketch lines and add color using the tools of your choice.

5

Shading in this drawing helps accentuate the folds and wrinkles in Arlo's clothing.

Arlo: Still Pose

Start with a circle and guidelines for the head and the face. Add vertical and horizontal axis lines and then draw circles for the joints. Rough in the details and use your eraser to remove old sketch lines.

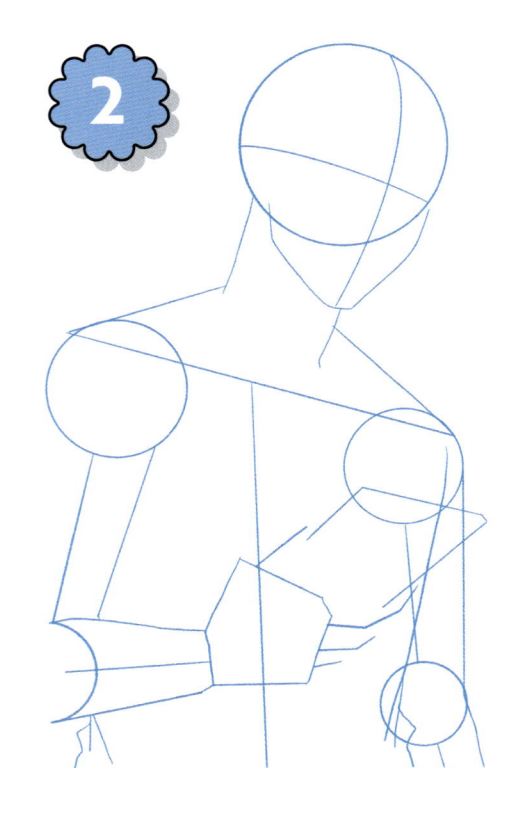

When you are satisfied with your drawing, add color using the tools of your choice.

4

5

Use shading to help add depth and dimension to Arlo's hair.

Remi: Head (Front View)

Begin with a circle. Add a vertical guideline marking the forward direction of the head and the face. Add horizontal guidelines to help determine where to place the features. Shape the chin and rough in the details.

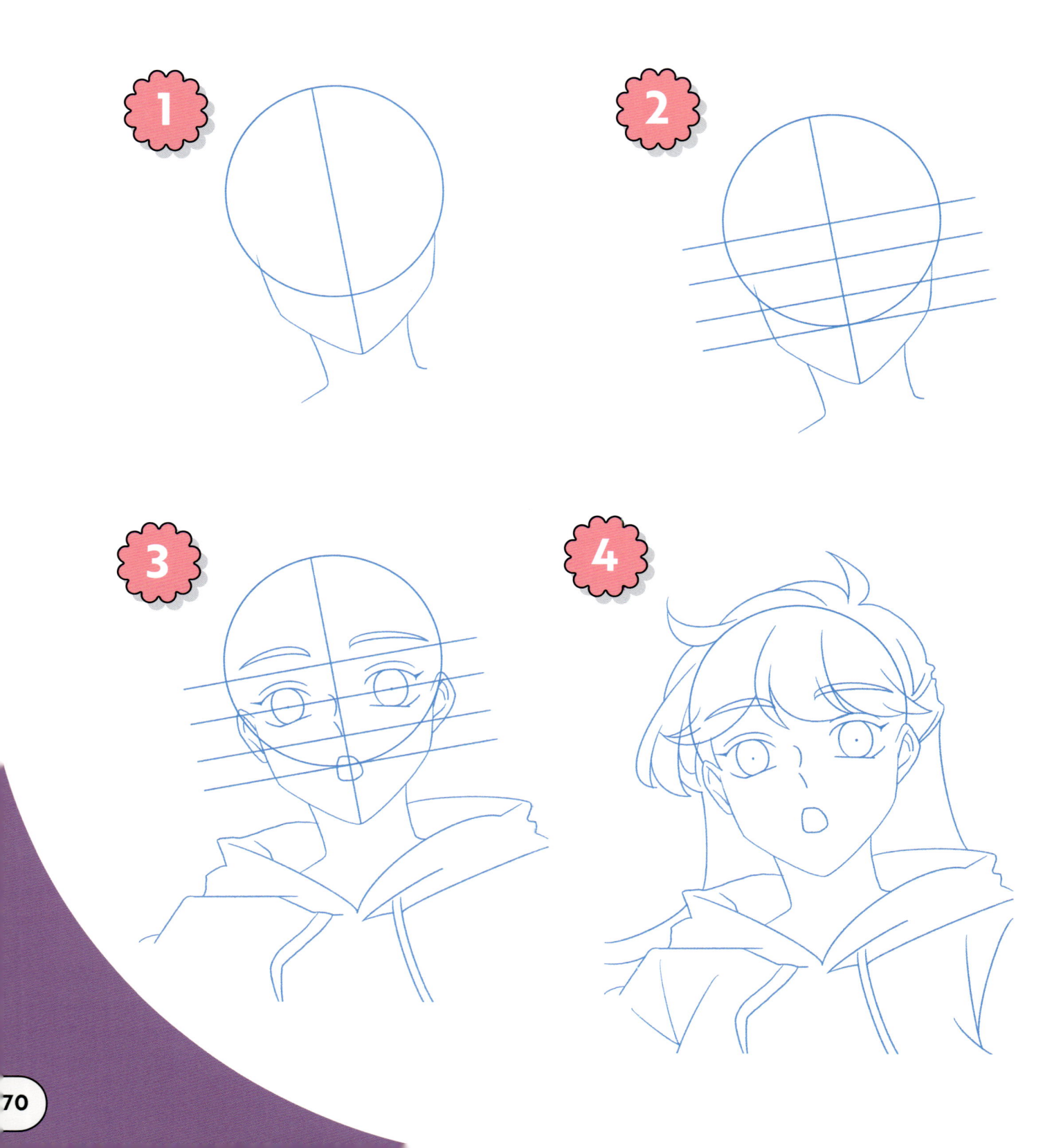

5

When you are satisfied with your drawing, add color using the tools of your choice.

6

An open mouth and wide eyes suggest a surprised or shocked expression.

Remi: Full Body (3/4 View)

Start with a circle for the head and guidelines for the face. Add vertical and horizontal axis lines; then denote the joints with circles and the feet with triangles. Follow the steps to fill in the details.

4

When you are satisfied with your drawing, add color using the tools of your choice.

5

A hand on the hip, one foot kicked out, and a mock salute adds fun and interest to the pose.

Blyke: Head (Front View)

Begin with a circle. Add a vertical guideline marking the forward direction of the head and the face. Add horizontal guidelines to help determine where to place the features. Shape the chin and rough in the details.

When you are satisfied with your drawing, erase any old sketch lines and add color using the tools of your choice.

Adding a white highlight to the eyes gives them an "alive" look and is just one of many details that will make your art look more polished.

Blyke: Dynamic Pose

Start with a circle, facial guidelines, and vertical and horizontal axis lines. Then, denote the joints with circles. Follow the steps to fill in the details.

4

When you are satisfied with your drawing, erase any old sketch lines and add color using the tools of your choice.

5

Use different shades of red, combined with white, to give Blyke's energy a dynamic vibe.

Blyke: Action Pose

Start with a circle and guidelines to establish the direction of the head and the face. Add horizontal and vertical axis lines that show this body in motion. Denote the joints with circles and the left foot with a triangle. Build out the form and rough in the details. This is a challenging pose, but keep at it!

4

When you are satisfied with your drawing, erase any old sketch lines and add color using the tools of your choice.

5

The two balls of energy under Blyke's hands also emphasize the movement of the pose.

Isen: Head (Front View)

Begin with a circle. Add a vertical guideline marking the forward direction of the head and the face. Add horizontal guidelines to help determine where to place the features. Rough in the shape of the chin and complete the details.

5

When you are satisfied with your drawing, erase any old sketch lines and add color using the tools of your choice.

6

While still angular, Isen's face and jaw are a bit softer than some of the other characters' faces.

Isen: Full Body (3/4 View)

Start with a circle for the head and guidelines for the face. Add vertical and horizontal axis lines; then denote the joints with circles and use triangles for the feet. Follow the steps to fill in the details.

4

When you are satisfied with your drawing, erase any old sketch lines and add color using the tools of your choice.

5

A bend in the knee, one foot kicked back, and slightly splayed arms shows Isen in a walking pose.

Isen: Static Pose

Start with a circle and guidelines for the head and the face.
Add vertical and horizontal axis lines and then draw circles
for the joints. Rough in the details and then use your eraser to
remove old sketch lines as you draw.

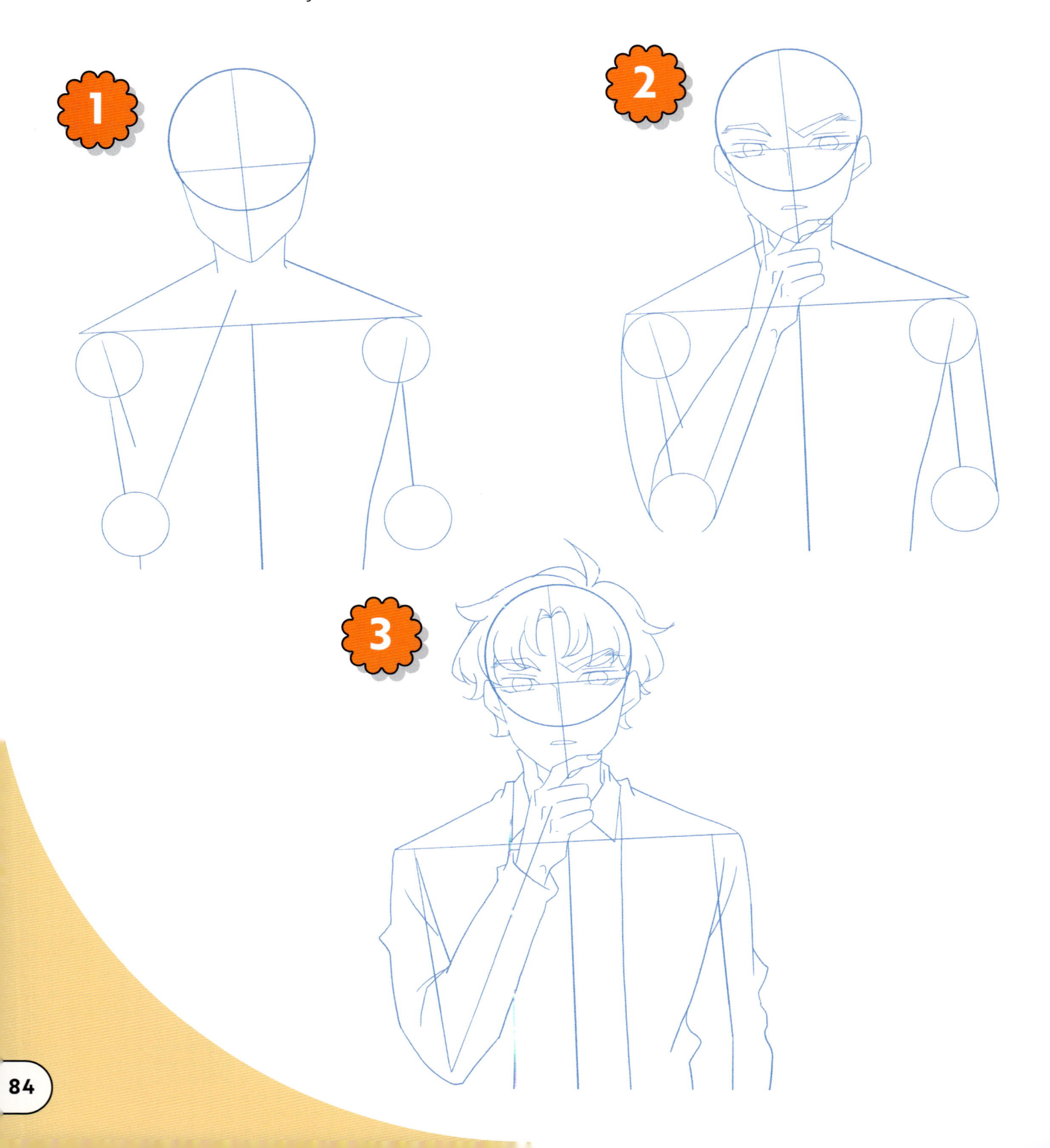

4

When you are satisfied with your drawing, erase any old sketch lines and add color using the tools of your choice.

5

A hand holding the chin suggests a character who is contemplating something or possibly confused.

Clothing, Props, and Accessories

Even though some characters wear signature outfits, there will always be opportunities to change their core pieces, particularly if they are important to the storyline or character in the course of your webcomic series.

Try drawing your characters in various scenes and situations. Think about what they might wear as well as what props and accessories might be required in the scenes to move the storyline forward in a meaningful way.

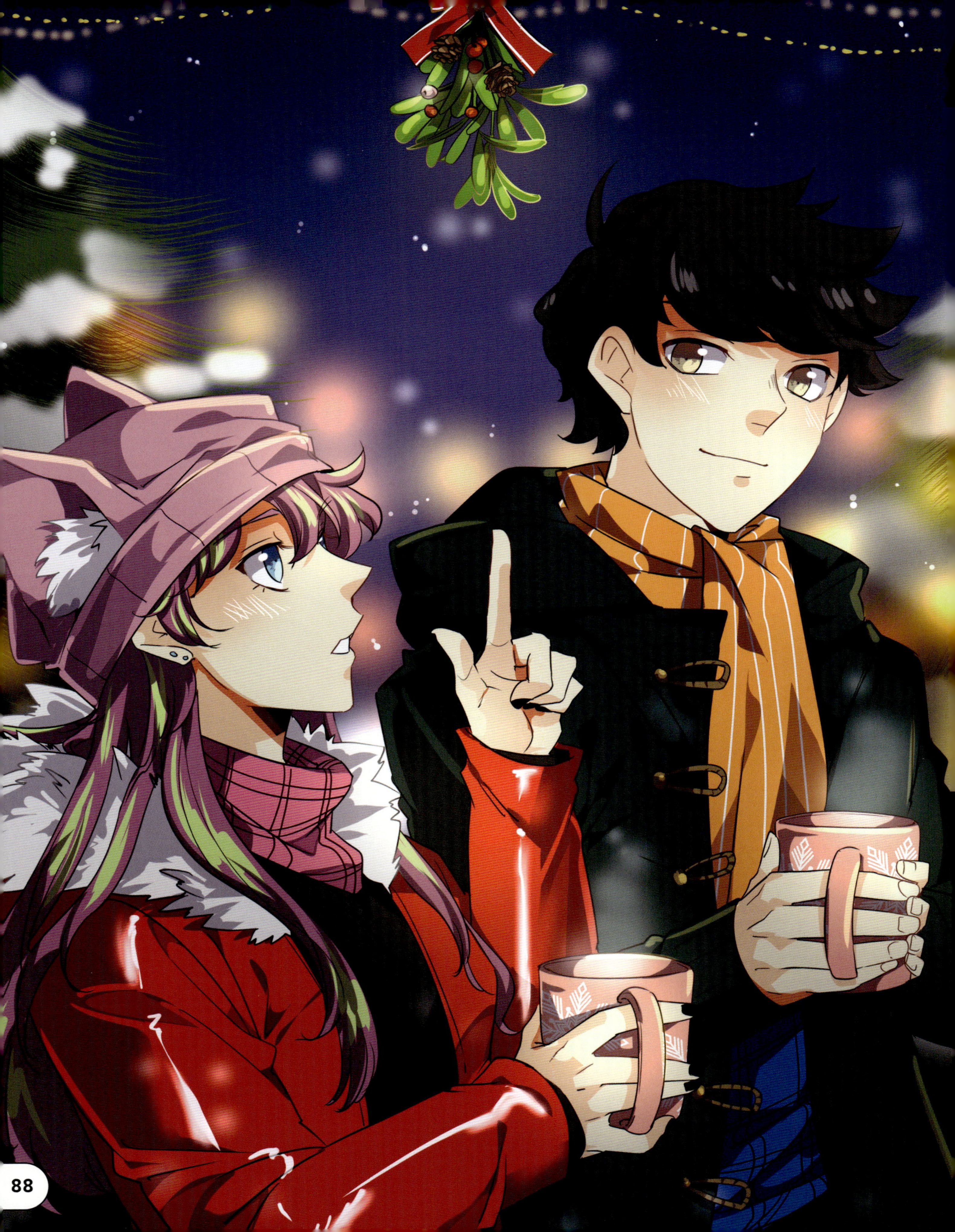

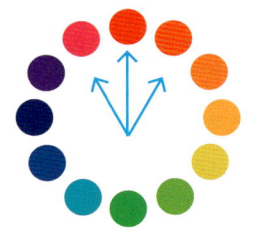

ANALOGOUS:
THREE COLORS
NEXT TO EACH
OTHER

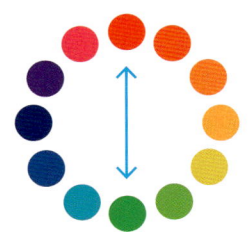

COMPLEMENTARY:
OPPOSITES ON THE
COLOR WHEEL

Adding Color

A color wheel can be divided into categories: primary, secondary, tertiary, complementary, and analogous colors. Red, yellow, and blue are primary colors, and the rest are derived from various mixtures of these primaries. A complementary color offers the most contrast to its matching primary color.

When illustrating scenes, think about tone, saturation, and contrast. Think about your characters and how colors can enhance their personalities, actions, and abilities.

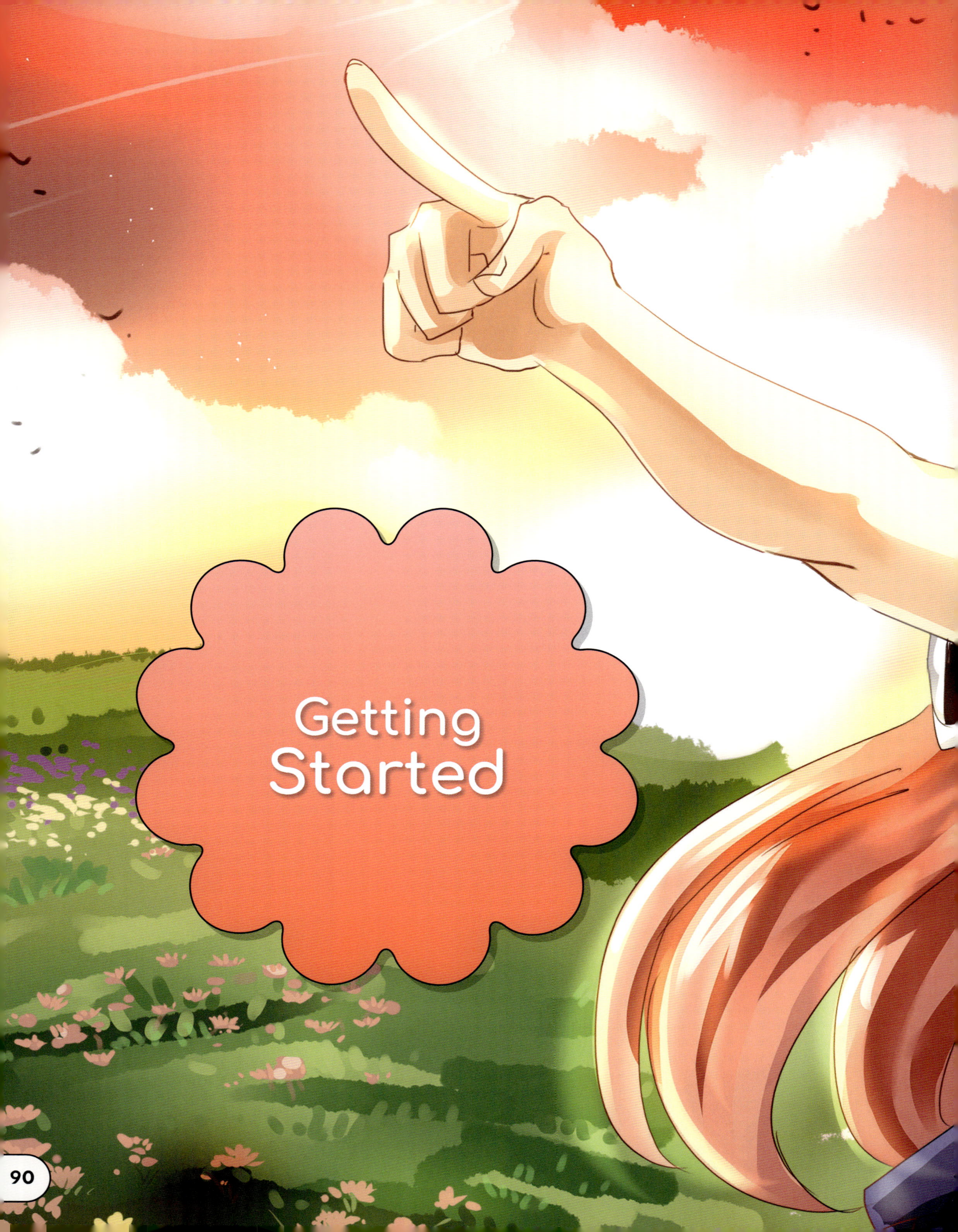

Getting Started

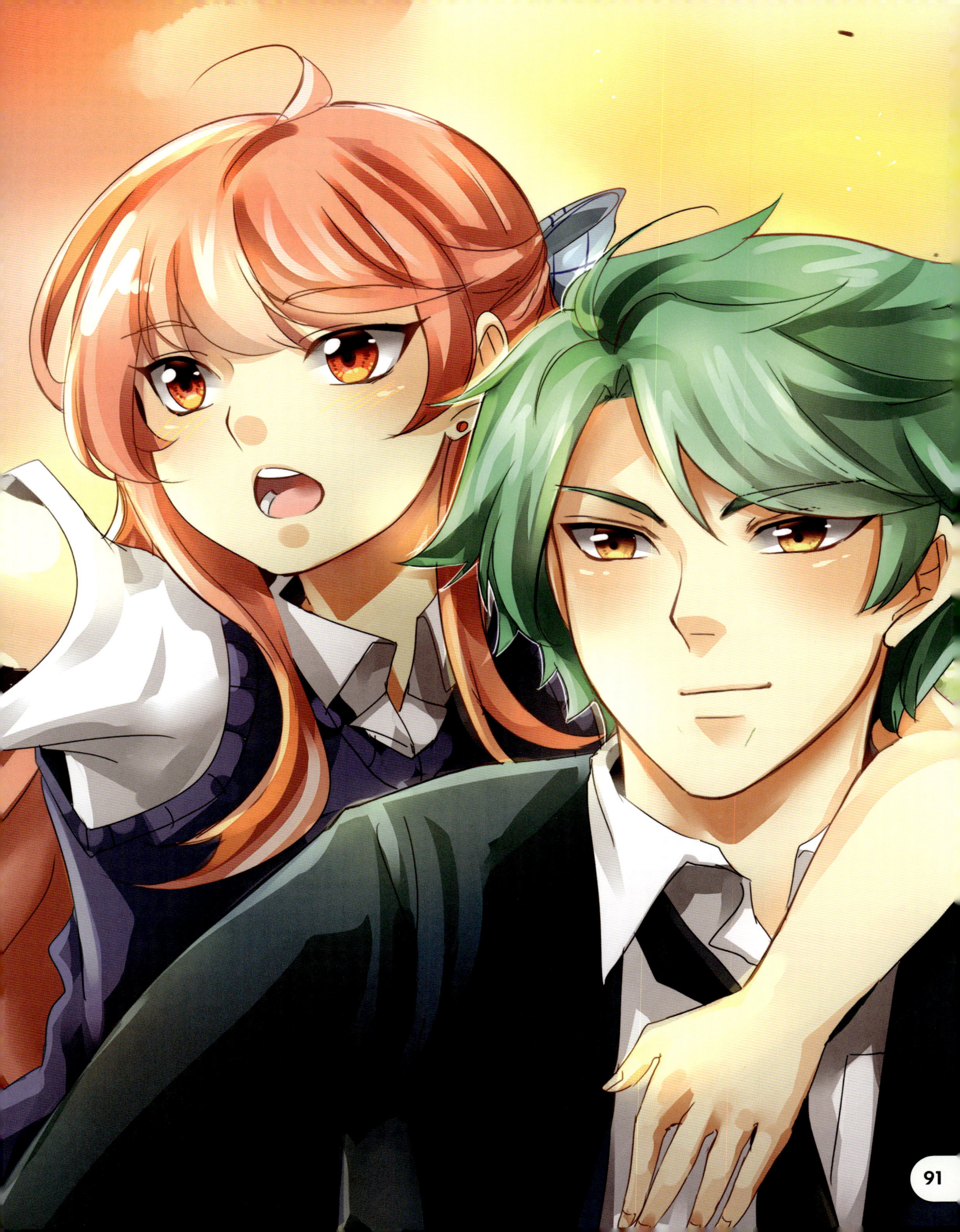

Introduction to Publishing on WEBTOON

WEBTOON introduced a new way to create stories for anyone who has a story to tell. If you want to publish your own webcomic, your story can start with CANVAS, WEBTOON's self- publishing platform.

Posting on CANVAS means that you, as a creator, have control over all aspects of your story and can use the platform to build a unique audience thanks to the thousands of readers that visit the platform daily.

Some of WEBTOON's most popular titles began on WEBTOON CANVAS. WEBTOON Originals are stories that are developed for the platform.

Unlike traditional comics, which are meant to be read in a print format, WEBTOON is a mobile-based platform, so the content has been formatted to be read vertically.

Through the vertical format, reading a WEBTOON series is meant to feel like a cinematic experience since the reader can see only one panel at a time instead of the entire page like in a traditional print comic.

If you have a story to tell and want to create your own webcomic, it takes planning.

DEVELOP YOUR CHARACTERS

Creating believable characters is one of the most important tasks for any creator. When developing a character for your story, consider these parameters in order to have a good understanding of who they are; this will ground the character in your story and make them seem more believable to the reader:

- What is their role in the story?
- What is this character's intended arc? A character arc is usually the internal journey a character goes through over the course of the story.
- What are their strengths and weaknesses?
- What relationships do they have with other characters in the story?
- What is their motivation?

CREATE CHARACTER SHEETS

- Character Designs / Physical
- Characteristics / Color Palette
- Motivations (Wants vs. Needs)
- Mannerisms, Perks, and Flaws
- Circle of Being (Backstory)

PLAN YOUR STORY

What is the setting?

This is the location of the action that includes time and place (when and where).

What is the overall plot of your story?

The plot is the actual story. A plot should have a beginning, middle, and end, with a clear conflict and resolution:

- Conflict is usually a problem the plot is intended to resolve; without conflict, there's no story to tell.
- Resolution is the solution to the main conflict of the story. It's important to make sure the resolution feels earned by wrapping up the main story conflict, character arcs, and setting.

CREATE YOUR COMIC

THUMBNAILS

This is when you plan out your panels based on your story. Thumbnails are intended to be very loose, simple drawings that will help you have an understanding of how the episode will be structured. Storyboarding an episode can help creators plan scenes and sequences with pacing, clarity, and readability in mind for readers.

SKETCHES

Once you've created your rough thumbnails, you're ready to start sketching your characters and backgrounds. This is also the stage when creators plan out the placement of their speech bubbles.

INKING

Inking is the process of cleaning up your lines to create a more polished look.

COLORING & FINALIZING

Add color, speech bubbles, special effects, and lettering.

Developing a Scene

There are many ways to develop a scene in webcomics. You will want to experiment with what works best for your story, art, and style; however, there are some general guidelines that will help you get started. The important thing is to stay patient throughout the process and not get overwhelmed by making your scene "perfect" on the first try. This is your opportunity to experiment with composition, color, and other details that will add to a dynamic story.

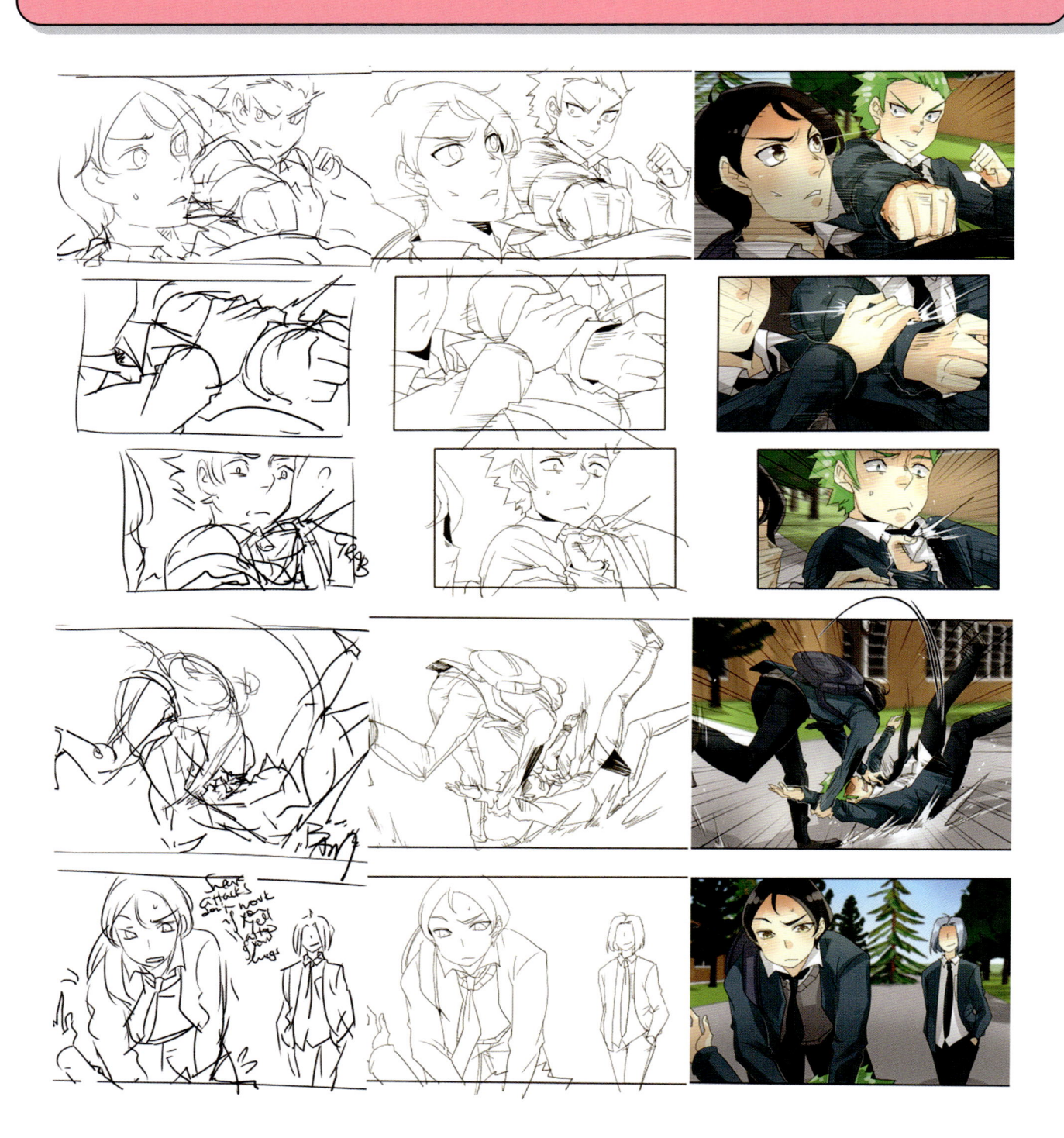

Below is an example of a completed scene from start to finish.

THUMBNAIL

COLORING

SKETCHING AND INKING

ADDING THE DETAILS

About the Creator

uru-chan (Chelsey Han) grew up in Acton, Massachusetts. She has always had a love for manga and anime, eventually teaching herself how to draw and write her own stories. As a teen, she enjoyed posting short comics online for others to read. Now, she's delighted that so many fans connect with the characters of unOrdinary. She hopes this book can be helpful to those who want to bring their own characters to life.

For more from uru-chan, check out:
X (formerly Twitter): @uruchanOFR
Instagram: @uru.chan
TikTok: @uruchanofficial